EXILES-A PLAY IN THREE ACTS

James Joyce

Originally published: 1918

Genres: Drama

Biography of James Joyce

James Augustine Aloysius Joyce was born on February 2, 1882, just south of Dublin in a wealthy suburb called Rathgar. The Joyce family was initially well off as Dublin merchants with bloodlines that connected them to old Irish nobility in the country. James' father, John Joyce, was a fierce Irish Catholic patriot and his political and religious influences are most evident in Joyce's two key works A Portrait of the Artist as a Young Man and Ulysses.

As a result of their steadily diminishing wealth and income, the Joyce family was repeatedly forced to move to more modest residences and John Joyce's habitual unemployment as well as his drinking and spending habits, made it difficult for the Joyces to retain their previous social standing. A young James Joyce was sent away to the renowned Clongowes School in 1888?a Jesuit institution that was regarded as the best preparatory school in Ireland. The Clongowes school figures prominently in Joyce's work, specifically in the story of his recurring character Stephen Dedalus. Joyce earned high marks both at the Clongowes School and at Belvedere College in Dublin where he continued. At this point in his life, it seemed evident that Joyce was to enter the priesthood, a decision that would have pleased his parents. As James Joyce made contact with various members of the "Irish Literary Renaissance," his interest in the priesthood waned. Indeed, Joyce became increasingly critical of Ireland and its conservative elements, especially the Church.

In opposition to his mother's wishes, Joyce left Ireland in 1902 to pursue a medical education in Paris, and did not return to Ireland until the following year upon news of his mother's debilitation and imminent death. After burying his mother, Joyce continued in Ireland, working as a schoolteacher at a boys' school?another autobiographical detail that recurs in the story of Stephen Dedalus. After barely spending a year in Dublin, Joyce returned to the Continent, drifting in and out of medical school in Paris before taking up residence in Zurich. It was during this period that Joyce began writing professionally.

In 1905, Joyce completed a collection of eight stories, entitled Dubliners, though it was not until 1913 that the volume was actually printed. During these frustrating and impoverished years, Joyce heavily relied upon the emotional support of Nora Barnacle, his unmarried Irish lover, as well as the financial support of his younger brother, Stanislaus Joyce. Both Nora and Stanislaus remained as protective, supporting figures for the duration of the writer's life. During the eight years between Dubliners' completion and publication, Joyce and Barnacle had two children, a son named Giorgio and a daughter named Lucia.

Joyce's next major work, A Portrait of the Artist as a Young Man, appeared in serialized form in 1914 and 1915, before Joyce was "discovered" by Ezra Pound and the complete text was printed in New York in 1916, and in London in 1917. It was with the assistance of Pound, a prominent literary figure of the time, that Joyce came in contact with Harriet Shaw Weaver, who served as both editor and patron while Joyce wrote Ulysses.

When Ulysses was published in Paris in 1922, many immediately hailed the work as genius. With his inventive narrative style and engagement with multiple philosophical themes, Joyce had established himself as a leading Modernist. The novel charts the passage of one day?June, 16 1904?as depicted in the life of an Irish Jew named Leopold Bloom, who plays the role of a Ulysses by wandering through the streets of Dublin. Despite the fact that Joyce was writing in self-imposed exile, living in Paris, Zurich and Trieste while writing Ulysses, the novel is noted for the incredible amount of accuracy and detail regarding the physical and geographical features of Dublin.

Thematically similar to Joyce's previous works, Ulysses examines the relationship between the modern man and his myth and history, focusing on contemporary questions of Irish political and cultural independence, the effects of organized religion on the soul, and the cultural and moral decay produced economic development and heightened urbanization. While Joyce was writing the epic work, there was serious doubt as to whether Ulysses would be completed. Midway through his writing, Joyce suffered the first of eleven eye operations to salvage his ever-worsening eyesight. At one point, a disappointed Joyce cast the bulk of his manuscript into the fire, though Nora Barnacle immediately rescued it.

While Ulysses was hailed by some, the novel was banned from both the United Kingdom as well as the United States on obscenity charges. It was not until 1934, that Random House won a court battle that granted permission to print and distribute Joyce's Ulysses in the United States; two years later, the novel was legalized in Britain.

By that time, Joyce was approaching the end of his public career having concluded his work on a final novel entitled Finnegan's Wake. Considered to be far more baffling and convoluted than Ulysses, Finnegan's Wake was a critical failure, ostracizing Joyce from many of his former admirers. At the outbreak of World War II, Joyce remained in Paris until he was forced to move?first to Vichy and then to Switzerland. On January 13, 1941, James Joyce died of a stomach ulcer at the age of 58, and was buried in Zurich's

Fluntern Cemetery. Though his prestige had faded towards the end of his life, Joyce regained literary stature in the decades following his death and Ulysses now stands as the definitive text of the Anglo-American modernist movement, marking Joyce's creative genius and premier abilities as a stylist of the English language.

Exiles Background

Exiles is a written play by James Joyce that includes three acts; the manuscript was written in 1914, finished in 1915, and published in 1918. Despite the efforts made by Joyce and American poet and critic Ezra Pound, to whom Joyce had shown the manuscript prior to his publication, the play was rejected to be produced; it was however rediscovered in 1970 and made into a London play (directed by Harold Pinter). The plot of the story revolves around a complicated love affair of a man (Robert) that meets a married woman (Bertha) who he used to love, and her husband (Richard) who he used to drink alcohol with. The major point of the play is the sense of doubt about what occurred between Acts Two and Three, the uncertainty about whether the affair between Robert and Bertha has actually happened or not.

James Joyce was born in 1882 in Ireland, and is best known for his poetry, short stories, and novels. *Exiles* is the only play that he has written, making it unique in its conjugation. It draws a parallel with Joyce's life with his lover Nora Barnacle: the two lived, unmarried, in Trieste, and they considered themselves to be living "in exile" - it is not, however, an autobiographical play.

The writing style and content of *Exiles* looks back to "The Dead", the final short story in the 1914 short-stories collection *Dubliners*, and forward to *Ulysses*, the modernist novel which Joyce began around the time of the composition of *Exiles* (1914) and published on February 2, 1922 (the day of his 40th birthday).

xiles Themes

Jealousy and Suspicion

The entire plot of *Exiles* is colored by jealousy and suspicion. Rowan is placed in a situation where he's sorely tempted by these feelings because of the untrustworthy behavior of his wife and friend. Together they hatch a scheme which both involved Rowan and denies him the opportunity to remain knowledgeable about the affair. By asking for his opinion, Bertha makes Rowan a sort of accomplice in his own cuckolding. If he refuses, then she will most likely call him a tyrant, but if he encourages her, then he somehow accepts responsibility for any potential emotional damage as a result of the affair. Washing his hands of any involvement, Rowan is shut out in the dark. He becomes consumed by jealousy, waking early the next morning and heading to town. He confronts Hand, but he makes little progress because his friend fabricates an elaborate lie about the previous evening. By the time he returns home, Rowan is even more deceived than when he initially was approached by Bertha. He tells his wife that he's willing to forgive and move on, but his trust in her is severely damaged. He will forevermore doubt the sincerity of her love as well as her loyalty. His suspicion is not unfounded, but justified under the circumstances; he's paranoid but for good reason.

Rejection

Rowan's character is defined by the rejection with which he is treated throughout the play. Even from the start, he is leaving his home of several years, Rome. Before that he left Ireland in order to establish himself as a writer, something he was unable to accomplish among his childhood peers. By the time Bertha approaches him with Hand's advances at the dinner party, Rowan has become firmly defined by his relationship to rejection. Rather than offering an opinion, he places the decision squarely on her discernment. When Bertha does visit Hand's home, Rowan is already there. He had anticipated her choice and attempted to persuade his friend to respect the sanctity of their marriage. When Bertha walks in, she dismisses him. Once more and one final time Rowan is rejected, this time directly from his wife's will.

Subterfuge and Mystery

As far as the plot is concerned, the primary device to hold audience interest is subterfuge. The audience is never told whether or not Bertha and Hand have an affair. They are merely shown that Bertha visits his home on the night in question. This element of mystery both captures the audience's attention and allows them to identify and relate to Rowan. Because the audience only encounters information through Rowan's investigation, they are forced to recognize his plight of misinformation. By gradually revealing the complexity of the investigation, Joyce encouraged the audience to pay attention and to form their own conclusions and suspicions about the affair.

Exiles Literary Elements

Genere:

Drama

Language

English

Setting and Context

The action of the play is set sometimes in the 19th century and the action takes place over the course of a few days inside Richard's house.

Narrator and Point of View

Because this is a play, there is neither narrator nor a point of view from which the play is told from.

Tone and Mood

The tone and mood in the play is a tense one, created by the different sins and secrets kept hidden by the characters.

Protagonist and Antagonist

The protagonist is Richard and the antagonist is his dead mother, the person who could never accept her son for who he was.

Major Conflict

The major conflict is an internal one and is the result of Beatrice's incapability to choose between Richard and Robert.

Climax

The play reaches its climax when Richard and Bertha reconcile and decide to get over the problems in their relationship and that who they really want is one another.

Foreshadowing

The first act begins with a conversation between Beatrice and Brigid mentioning the weather, which was ''wet''. The mentioning of rain in the beginning of the play is used here to foreshadow the future turmoil the characters will have to go through.

Understatement

One of the biggest understatements in the play is the idea that Richard loved Beatrice and that Robert and Bertha are meant to be together. This is however proved to be not true as both Bertha and Richard express their desire to be with one another.

Allusions

One of the allusions made in the play in the second act is that Bertha and Robert had sex the night Bertha spent at Robert's house. While both character denied it, the possibility still remains and in fact Richard is convinced that Bertha had sex with his friend.

Imagery

An important imagery in the play is the way Protestantism is portrayed by the characters. Even though some of them admit they are religious people, they criticize Protestantism for being too righteous. What this description does is to portray the Protestant religion as an extremely strict religion which grounds its people into various doctrines and beliefs.

Paradox

A paradoxical idea is the way in which Beatrice treats her father's religion, Protestantism. In the beginning of the play, she expressed her belief that a person can find happiness only through religion and that she thought about going to a covenant and staying there in order to feel peaceful. However, when she talks about her father's religion, Protestantism, she is quick to judge it and to label it as something which has a negative influence of a person's life. This idea is paradoxical especially considering how much Beatrice tried to convince those around her that she wants to become involved in religion.

Parallelism

A parallel can be drawn between Bertha and Beatrice, in the sense they are both rather liberal women who do not limit themselves to only one man. Also, both women are outspoken, not fearing what others will think of them if they dare to speak their mind. However, what differs is the way they find happiness. In this sense, Beatrice differs a lot from Bertha because she does not have the strength to confess her feelings and to put herself in the position to be hurt.

Personification

No personification can be found in the play.

Use of Dramatic Devices

The narrator uses a multitude of dramatic devices in the play, starting from the First Act. For example, in the beginning of the first act, the narrator offers through the use of dramatic devices a very detailed description of the room where the action will take place. The narrator uses dramatic devices to signal the time and the manner when one character enters the room and another character leaves the room. The narrator also used dramatic devices to express the inner thoughts of various characters and also to present background information the reader of the person watching the play would not know otherwise.

Exiles Symbols, Allegory and Motifs

Symbol for the lack of independence a servant had

In the first Act, the servant in the house tells the master, Richard, that there are some letters in the mailbox which she would like to take out. Richard gives the servant the keys to the letterbox and the servant retrieves the letters. The lack of access to the letterbox is used in this Act as a symbol to suggest the lack of independence and influence a servant had in a household.

The outsider

Another common motif in the play is the idea that Richard always felt as if he was an outsider when it came to Beatrice and Robert. Richard expresses his feelings about the matter to Beatrice when they talk about a possible relationship between the two of them and Richard uses this occasion to express his feelings regarding the relationship Beatrice had with Robert.

Symbol for familiarity

It was uncommon for men and women from those times to be on a first name basis with other people, even with those around their age or even relatives. When someone called another person by their given name, it usually meant that those people were extremely close, probably married. The use of the first name becomes in this context a symbol used for familiarity and also to suggest that the two people using the names were extremely close.

All men are the same

One of the common motifs in the play is the idea that all men are the same. This idea is promoted by the women of the play who remind the males that no matter how hard they try to convince them that they are different, the women know that they had probably tried the same thing on other women as well. This becomes a common motif in the play, being repeated over and over again.

Symbol for a woman's obedience

When Richard comes home, he meets with Bertha and gives her his hat, instructing her to put it in the drawer. Bertha says nothing about the action, and choses to obey, even asking Richard if she is allowed to leave the room. This interaction is important because it shows just how submissive women were in those times. The hat also becomes a symbol in this case, used to show Bertha's submission when it comes to Richard.

Exiles Metaphors and Similes

Metaphor for his affection

When Beatrice returns to Richard, the latter asks her if she wants to read what he had written about her. Richard compares his writings with the sketches a painter may make of his loved one and can't understand why Beatrice would not like to see what he had written. The writings are used here as a metaphor to suggest the love Richard had for Beatrice and also his desire to be accepted by her.

Religion as a metaphor for peace

The idea transmitted by the characters in the play is that none of them are religious. Some religions, Protestantism for example, are harshly criticized by most of the characters but despite their dislike towards a certain religion, it is clear that most characters have a sort of respect for religious people and beliefs. More than once, characters such as Beatrice and Richard express their belief that the only way a person could find peace is through religion. Thus, because of this, religion becomes used in the play as a metaphor for lasting peace.

Harmonium

When Beatrice talks about the time she spent with her father, Robert intervenes and assumes that the time spent there could be compared with a melody played at the harmonium. The musical instrument mentioned here, harmonium, produces very somber notes and it is usually associated with sadness. Thus, what Robert wanted to highlight through this comparison is that Beatrice most likely did not enjoyed the time she spent at her father's house.

The piano

Beatrice is the only character in the play associated with the piano and apparently the only one who can play it. Throughout the play, whenever the musical instrument is mentioned, Beatrice appears as well. The fact that Beatrice can play the piano even though her parents are Protestants is interesting especially when considering how those who were Protestants did not saw music as a holy expression. Thus, the fact that Beatrice can play the piano is used as a metaphor to suggest her refusal to adhere to the social norms many would have liked to impose on her.

Like the moon

Robert talks with Bertha concerning the affection he had for her and he compares her with the moon. When Bertha asks him why he compares her with the moon, he claims it is because she is distant, beautiful and yet cold. This comparison is used in this context to characterize Bertha and to show just how much Robert was in love with her.

Exiles Irony

Not afraid of you

When Beatrice wants to go away, Richard convinces her to stay, and then asks her if she is afraid of him. Initially, Beatrice tries to convince him through her words that she was not afraid of him. Ironically, the description of her actions, the way she behaved when Richard tried to touch her proved the complete opposite.

You must ask me but it may be that I will not answer you

After being reunited with Beatrice, Richard asks her a number of questions, trying to find out what she was thinking about the relationship and what she wanted from a possible future relationship. Unfortunately, Beatrice refused to answer time and time again. When she was instead told to speak her mind, she told Richard he must continue to ask her questions, to which, ironically, she continued to give no clear answers.

You come to me but you still love another

When Beatrice first sees Richard after a long period of time, they discuss the former relationship Beatrice had with Robert. It is clear that the couple loved one another very much and it is possible that Beatrice still had feelings for Robert. Knowing this, it is ironic to see how she went to Richard, a man she knew that was in love with her.

I will leave you alone with him

Soon after the initial conversation between Richard and Beatrice, a knock was heard on the door. Upon hearing this, Richard was quick to excuse himself, claiming he did not want to stick around to meet with Robert. Thus, ironically, Richard let Beatrice in the hands of his most pertinent rival, even though he knew Beatrice still had feelings for Robert.

You say this to other women as well

When Robert tried to convince Bertha that he loves her, he used a lot of compliments and tried to convince her of his affections using flattering and also gifts. Robert hoped these actions will convince Bertha to give in and agree to be with him but ironically, it had the opposite effect. The reason why Robert's actions did not had the expected result was because Robert already used the same strategy with other women and thus became known because of this.

Exiles Imagery

Always together

In the first Act, Richard talks about the relationship Beatrice had with Robert and told her the way she saw them. Richard portrays the couple as being always together, inseparable even. From the way the couple is portrayed, it is transmitted the idea that Beatrice and Robert loved one another deeply and thus took advantage of every opportunity they could to be with one another.

The woman who can't decide what she wants

An important imagery which must be analyzed is the way in which Beatrice is portrayed. She is a woman loved by to men and it appears she loves the both men to some extent. Because of this, she finds it impossible to choose one man to be with and instead moves from one man to another, knowing that both will accept her because of their love. Her actions portray Beatrice as a capricious woman, someone who can't make up her mind and a woman who can cause a lot of pain.

Unloving mother

Richard portrays himself at times as being a difficult person, someone who has trouble understanding others and how the world works at times. As a way of explaining why Richard is the way he is, the mother of Richard is portrayed in less than stellar, as a judgmental and harsh woman who can't understand her son and who does not want to know why he behaved in a way she considered as being improper. The image portrayed here is that of a harsh mother and this is used in part to argue why Richard ended up as a dysfunctional adult.

Loving father

Another important image in the play is the way Richard portrays his own father, especially when comparing him with the image created about his mother. While the mother is presented as a ruthless woman, the father is imagined as sweet and generous, kind towards Richard up until his last day on this earth. The father died when Richard was only 14 years old and yet the image he kept in his heart was that of a man he will always respect and admire.

Exiles Characters

Richard Rowan

Rowan is a successful writer, the protagonist of the play. Having finished a book in Rome, he returns to his homeland, Ireland. Adapting to parenthood, he brings along his common-law wife, Bertha, and their son, Archie. Unwilling to stifle her autonomy, Rowan allows her to pursue an affair with his old friend, Robert Hand. As the play progresses, Rowan becomes increasingly jealous and suspicious of Bertha. Although he has given her freedom to make her choices without consulting him, he hopes that she remains true. After Hand publishes a particularly flattering review of Rowan's book, Rowan confronts his friend and rival. No progress is made, but he returns home to make amends with his "wife." Rowan's trust and ability to become vulnerable with her are severely damaged.

Bertha

Bertha becomes enchanted by Hand's advances over dinner. After asking Rowan whether or not she should pursue his old friend, she takes matters into her own hands. Bertha's primary conflict is against herself. She cannot decide which man she desires more, but her loyalty is questionable either way. By the end of the play her fidelity is still in question, never reaching a resolution. She does, however, persuade and benefit from Rowan's forgiveness and reconciliation.

Archie Rowan

Archie is Rowan's son with Bertha. He is very young and does not play a significant role in most of the play. He is described as an illegitimate son, making his status and affiliation somewhat vague. His parents give him very little concern or attention.

Beatrice Justice

Beatrice used to date Rowan when he lived in Ireland. Now she is dating Hand, Rowan's old friend. Her reappearance in Rowan's life is marked by awkwardness. No longer interested in her, Rowan treats her with timidity and distance. Without her knowledge, Hand flirts with Bertha, making her the only character left in the dark regarding the dinner party match-making.

Robert Hand

Having spent many fond years as a confidante and drinking partner with Rowan, Hand is an old friend. Upon meeting Bertha, however, he is willing to compromise that friendship for her affections. He seduces Bertha and invites her to his home after the dinner party. Although the nature of her visit remains a mystery, she leaves under a cloud of suspicion. Hand interacts with Rowan afterward as if he has everything to prove. He even writes a flattering newspaper article about his old friend, most likely in an attempt to help him forget the potential affair of the night before. When he meets with Rowan later, Hand fabricates an elaborate story of bringing an escort home with him after visiting a bar -- not Bertha. He demonstrates a sever lack of loyalty and honesty in his treatment of Rowan.

Exiles Summary

Act 1

Richard Rowan is an author hoping to establish his family in Ireland, his homeland, after spending some time overseas in Rome. He has brought his common-law wife, Bertha, and their son, Archie, with him. Upon returning to Ireland, he runs into an ex named Bertha and her current boyfriend and Richard's old pal, Robert Hand. Introductions aside, Robert makes a move on Bertha in Richard's home that evening. They kiss passionately for a while before he invites her over to his place later that night. Of course Bertha tells Richard about the advances, but she tells him she's considering the offer. Obviously jealous, he tells her to make her own decisions.

Act 2

Robert is patiently waiting in his home for Bertha's arrival, but he's surprised to see Richard. Richard confronts him about the seduction of his girlfriend. Suddenly Bertha arrives. Taking the message, Richard leaves her to her own affairs, returning home. Bertha spends some intimate, romantic time with Robert, but the audience is not informed whether or not they make love. Afterward she speaks fondly to him. He asks for a profession of love, however, which she is unwilling to make.

Act 3

Early the next morning Bertha awakens at home to the maid's announcement that Richard left the house early. He's gone for a walk to clear his head. Bertha notes an article in the paper written about Richard by Robert. Apparently he's decided to stroke Richard's ego by celebrating his return to Ireland. Both Robert and Bertha verbally agree that last night was a dream, but circumstances won't allow the audience to believe this. Robert visits Richard in order to persuade him that nothing happened the previous night between he and Bertha. He claims to have written that newspaper piece at home, picked up a woman at a nightclub, and spent the night with her. Although he does not profess belief in Robert's alibi, Richard returns home to Bertha and makes up with her. He confesses that last night he secretly wanted to feel cheated in order to revive a sense of passion and intrigue for her. In his arms Bertha confesses how badly she longs for her "lover," claiming it is Richard, but there is some obvious room for doubt in her profession.

Exiles Analysis

James Joyce is best known for his novels, epic in flavor, but before those successes he wrote his only play, *Exiles*. Treating the topics of jealousy, autonomy, and intimacy, Joyce writes about a man who watches his romantic relationship fall to pieces. The protagonist, Richard Rowan, bears striking parallels to Joyce himself, serving as an intermediary between audience and playwright.

Richard, having just finished writing a successful book, returns with his wife and son to his homeland, Ireland. After running into old acquaintances -- Beatrice and Robert -- who are now dating one another, the two couples decide to dine together in Richard's home. By the end of the night, Beatrice, Richard's wife, has told him that Robert has invited her to his home for a late-night rendezvous. The sexual implications are strong. Although the truth of that night is never revealed, Richard awakens early to wrestle through his jealousy and suspicion over his wife's likely affair. He confronts Robert, but Robert invents a plausible alibi. Finally Richard returns home to <u>Bertha</u> and chooses to extend forgiveness without pressing the matter further, but his trust in her is severely compromised. Now he's a single man living a lie, no longer willing to engage in vulnerability with Bertha.

The parallels between Joyce's life and Richard's cannot be ignored. First of all, both men are Irish authors. Based upon these qualities alone, the audience can suppose that Joyce is drawing upon personal experience to inspire Richard's character. Struggling with his romantic relationships throughout his life, Joyce would have had ample material from which to draw for sourcing his play. He would have been no stranger to jealousy and humiliation.

Following this connection between playwright and protagonist, the audience is left with some disturbing conclusions. Richard's behavior in response to Beatrice and Robert reflects a certain degree of masochism. Rather than offering his own opinions, he demands that Beatrice make her own decisions. Surely this reflects a feminist issue of empowerment, but it also demonstrates his judgmental nature. He refuses to act as Beatrice's conscience, instead preferring to willingly allow her to betray him. If she could do it, then he wants to know. He forces the same sort of decision upon her in the third act, making her the judge between Robert and himself. In fact, Robert accuses his friend of setting him up at dinner by seeing the dangerous waters which Robert was treading with Beatrice but not saying anything to prevent the affair.

Doubtless born out of a deeply suspicious nature and self-hatred, Richard forces the people closest to him into compromising situations, as if to test their loyalty. When they fail, he receives all the confirmation he needs to play the victim about his situation, proving to himself that he is unlovable. Bearing in mind Joyce's possible identification with the protagonist, then the reader must understand that Joyce has struggled with similar patterns, abusing his intelligence in order to test his loved ones.

First Act

The drawingroom in Richard Rowan's house at Merrion, a suburb of Dublin. On the right, forward, a fireplace, before which stands a low screen. Over the mantelpiece a giltframed glass. Further back in the right wall, folding doors leading to the parlour and kitchen. In the wall at the back to the right a small door leading to a study. Left of this a sideboard. On the wall above the sideboard a framed crayon drawing of a young man. More to the left double doors with glass panels leading out to the garden. In the wall at the left a window looking out on the road. Forward in the same wall a door leading to the hall and the upper part of the house. Between the window and door a lady's davenport stands against the wall. Near it a wicker chair. In the centre of the room a round table. Chairs, upholstered in faded green plush, stand round the table. To the right, forward, a smaller table with a smoking service on it. Near it an easychair and a lounge. Cocoanut mats lie before the fireplace, beside the lounge and before the doors. The floor is of stained planking. The double doors at the back and the folding doors at the right have lace curtains, which are drawn halfway. The lower sash of the window is lifted and the window is hung with heavy green plush curtains. The blind is pulled down to the edge of the lifted lower sash. It is a warm afternoon in June and the room is filled with soft sunlight which is waning.

[BRIGID *and* BEATRICE JUSTICE *come in by the door on the left.* BRIGID *is an elderly woman, lowsized, with irongrey hair.* BEATRICE JUSTICE *is a slender dark young woman of 27 years. She wears a wellmade navyblue costume and an elegant simply trimmed black straw hat, and carries a small portfolioshaped handbag.*]

BRIGID.
The mistress and Master Archie is at the bath. They never expected you. Did you send word you were back, Miss Justice?

BEATRICE.
No. I arrived just now.

BRIGID.
[*Points to the easychair.*] Sit down and I'll tell the master you are here. Were you long in the train?

BEATRICE.
[*Sitting down.*] Since morning.

BRIGID.
Master Archie got your postcard with the views of Youghal. You're tired out, I'm sure.

BEATRICE.
O, no. [*She coughs rather nervously.*] Did he practise the piano while I was away?

BRIGID.
[*Laughs heartily.*] Practice, how are you! Is it Master Archie? He is mad after the milkman's horse now. Had you nice weather down there, Miss Justice?

BEATRICE.
Rather wet, I think.

BRIGID.
[*Sympathetically.*] Look at that now. And there is rain overhead too. [*Moving towards the study.*] I'll tell him you are here.

BEATRICE.
Is Mr Rowan in?

BRIGID.
[*Points.*] He is in his study. He is wearing himself out about something he is writing. Up half the night he does be. [*Going.*] I'll call him.

BEATRICE.
Don't disturb him, Brigid. I can wait here till they come back if they are not long.

BRIGID.
And I saw something in the letterbox when I was letting you in. [*She crosses to the study door, opens it slightly and calls.*] Master Richard, Miss Justice is here for Master Archie's lesson.

[RICHARD ROWAN *comes in from the study and advances towards* BEATRICE, *holding out his hand. He is a tall athletic young man of a rather lazy carriage. He has light brown hair and a moustache and wears glasses. He is dressed in loose lightgrey tweed.*]

RICHARD.
Welcome.

BEATRICE.
[*Rises and shakes hands, blushing slightly.*] Good afternoon, Mr Rowan. I did not want Brigid to disturb you.

RICHARD.
Disturb me? My goodness!

BRIGID.
There is something in the letterbox, sir.

RICHARD.
[*Takes a small bunch of keys from his pocket and hands them to her.*] Here.

[BRIGID *goes out by the door at the left and is heard opening and closing the box. A short pause. She enters with two newspapers in her hands.*]

RICHARD.
Letters?

BRIGID.
No, sir. Only them Italian newspapers.

RICHARD.
Leave them on my desk, will you?

[BRIGID *hands him back the keys, leaves the newspapers in the study, comes out again and goes out by the folding doors on the right.*]

RICHARD.
Please, sit down. Bertha will be back in a moment.

[BEATRICE *sits down again in the easychair.* RICHARD *sits beside the table.*]

RICHARD.
I had begun to think you would never come back. It is twelve days since you were here.

BEATRICE.
I thought of that too. But I have come.

RICHARD.
Have you thought over what I told you when you were here last?

BEATRICE.
Very much.

RICHARD.
You must have known it before. Did you? [*She does not answer.*] Do you blame me?

BEATRICE.
No.

RICHARD.
Do you think I have acted towards you—badly? No? Or towards anyone?

BEATRICE.
[*Looks at him with a sad puzzled expression.*] I have asked myself that question.

RICHARD.
And the answer?

BEATRICE.
I could not answer it.

RICHARD.
If I were a painter and told you I had a book of sketches of you you would not think it so strange, would you?

BEATRICE.
It is not quite the same case, is it?

RICHARD.
[*Smiles slightly.*] Not quite. I told you also that I would not show you what I had written unless you asked to see it. Well?

BEATRICE.
I will not ask you.

RICHARD.
[*Leans forward, resting his elbows on his knees, his hands joined.*] Would you like to see it?

BEATRICE.
Very much.

RICHARD.
Because it is about yourself?

BEATRICE.
Yes. But not only that.

RICHARD.
Because it is written by me? Yes? Even if what you would find there is sometimes cruel?

BEATRICE.
[*Shyly.*] That is part of your mind, too.

RICHARD.
Then it is my mind that attracts you? Is that it?

BEATRICE.
[*Hesitating, glances at him for an instant.*] Why do you think I come here?

RICHARD.
Why? Many reasons. To give Archie lessons. We have known one another so many years, from childhood, Robert, you and I—haven't we? You have always been interested in me, before I went away and while I was away. Then our letters to each other about my book. Now it is published. I am here again. Perhaps you feel that some new thing is gathering in my brain; perhaps you feel that you should know it. Is that the reason?

BEATRICE.
No.

RICHARD.
Why, then?

BEATRICE.
Otherwise I could not see you.

[*She looks at him for a moment and then turns aside quickly.*]

RICHARD.
[*After a pause repeats uncertainly.*] Otherwise you could not see me?

BEATRICE.
[*Suddenly confused.*] I had better go. They are not coming back. [*Rising.*] Mr Rowan, I must go.

RICHARD.
[*Extending his arms.*] But you are running away. Remain. Tell me what your words mean. Are you afraid of me?

BEATRICE.
[*Sinks back again.*] Afraid? No.

RICHARD.
Have you confidence in me? Do you feel that you know me?

BEATRICE.
[*Again shyly.*] It is hard to know anyone but oneself.

RICHARD.
Hard to know me? I sent you from Rome the chapters of my book as I wrote them; and letters for nine long years. Well, eight years.

BEATRICE.
Yes, it was nearly a year before your first letter came.

RICHARD.
It was answered at once by you. And from that on you have watched me in my struggle. [*Joins his hands*

earnestly.] Tell me, Miss Justice, did you feel that what you read was written for your eyes? Or that you inspired me?

BEATRICE.
[*Shakes her head.*] I need not answer that question.

RICHARD.
What then?

BEATRICE.
[*Is silent for a moment.*] I cannot say it. You yourself must ask me, Mr Rowan.

RICHARD.
[*With some vehemence.*] Then that I expressed in those chapters and letters, and in my character and life as well, something in your soul which you could not— pride or scorn?

BEATRICE.
Could not?

RICHARD.
[*Leans towards her.*] Could not because you dared not. Is that why?

BEATRICE.
[*Bends her head.*] Yes.

RICHARD.
On account of others or for want of courage—which?

BEATRICE.
[*Softly.*] Courage.

RICHARD.
[*Slowly.*] And so you have followed me with pride and scorn also in your heart?

BEATRICE.
And loneliness.

[*She leans her head on her hand, averting her face.*
RICHARD *rises and walks slowly to the window on the left.*
He looks out for some moments and then returns towards
her, crosses to the lounge and sits down near her.]

RICHARD.
Do you love him still?

BEATRICE.
I do not even know.

RICHARD.
It was that that made me so reserved with you—then—
even though I felt your interest in me, even though I felt
that I too was something in your life.

BEATRICE.
You were.

RICHARD.
Yet that separated me from you. I was a third person, I
felt. Your names were always spoken together, Robert
and Beatrice, as long as I can remember. It seemed to
me, to everyone...

BEATRICE.
We are first cousins. It is not strange that we were often
together.

RICHARD.
He told me of your secret engagement with him. He had
no secrets from me; I suppose you know that.

BEATRICE.
[*Uneasily.*] What happened—between us—is so long
ago. I was a child.

RICHARD.
[*Smiles maliciously.*] A child? Are you sure? It was in the garden of his mother's house. No? [*He points towards the garden.*] Over there. You plighted your troth, as they say, with a kiss. And you gave him your garter. Is it allowed to mention that?

BEATRICE.
[*With some reserve.*] If you think it worthy of mention.

RICHARD.
I think you have not forgotten it. [*Clasping his hands quietly.*] I do not understand it. I thought, too, that after I had gone... Did my going make you suffer?

BEATRICE.
I always knew you would go some day. I did not suffer; only I was changed.

RICHARD.
Towards him?

BEATRICE.
Everything was changed. His life, his mind, even, seemed to change after that.

RICHARD.
[*Musing.*] Yes. I saw that you had changed when I received your first letter after a year; after your illness, too. You even said so in your letter.

BEATRICE.
It brought me near to death. It made me see things differently.

RICHARD.
And so a coldness began between you, little by little. Is that it?

BEATRICE.
[*Half closing her eyes.*] No. Not at once. I saw in him a pale reflection of you: then that too faded. Of what good is it to talk now?

RICHARD.
[*With a repressed energy.*] But what is this that seems to hang over you? It cannot be so tragic.

BEATRICE.
[*Calmly.*] O, not in the least tragic. I shall become gradually better, they tell me, as I grow older. As I did not die then they tell me I shall probably live. I am given life and health again—when I cannot use them. [*Calmly and bitterly.*] I am convalescent.

RICHARD.
[*Gently.*] Does nothing then in life give you peace? Surely it exists for you somewhere.

BEATRICE.
If there were convents in our religion perhaps there. At least, I think so at times.

RICHARD.
[*Shakes his head.*] No, Miss Justice, not even there. You could not give yourself freely and wholly.

BEATRICE.
[*Looking at him.*] I would try.

RICHARD.
You would try, yes. You were drawn to him as your mind was drawn towards mine. You held back from him. From me, too, in a different way. You cannot give yourself freely and wholly.

BEATRICE.
[*Joins her hands softly.*] It is a terribly hard thing to do,

Mr Rowan—to give oneself freely and wholly—and be happy.

RICHARD.
But do you feel that happiness is the best, the highest that we can know?

BEATRICE.
[*With fervour.*] I wish I could feel it.

RICHARD.
[*Leans back, his hands locked together behind his head.*] O, if you knew how I am suffering at this moment! For your case, too. But suffering most of all for my own. [*With bitter force.*] And how I pray that I may be granted again my dead mother's hardness of heart! For some help, within me or without, I must find. And find it I will.

[BEATRICE *rises, looks at him intently, and walks away toward the garden door. She turns with indecision, looks again at him and, coming back, leans over the easychair.*]

BEATRICE.
[*Quietly.*] Did she send for you before she died, Mr Rowan?

RICHARD.
[*Lost in thought.*] Who?

BEATRICE.
Your mother.

RICHARD.
[*Recovering himself, looks keenly at her for a moment.*] So that, too, was said of me here by my friends—that she sent for me before she died and that I did not go?

BEATRICE.
Yes.

RICHARD.
[*Coldly.*] She did not. She died alone, not having forgiven me, and fortified by the rites of holy church.

BEATRICE.
Mr Rowan, why did you speak to me in such a way?

RICHARD.
[*Rises and walks nervously to and fro.*] And what I suffer at this moment you will say is my punishment.

BEATRICE.
Did she write to you? I mean before...

RICHARD.
[*Halting.*] Yes. A letter of warning, bidding me break with the past, and remember her last words to me.

BEATRICE.
[*Softly.*] And does death not move you, Mr Rowan? It is an end. Everything else is so uncertain.

RICHARD.
While she lived she turned aside from me and from mine. That is certain.

BEATRICE.
From you and from...?

RICHARD.
From Bertha and from me and from our child. And so I waited for the end as you say; and it came.

BEATRICE.
[*Covers her face with her hands.*] O, no. Surely no.

RICHARD.
[*Fiercely.*] How can my words hurt her poor body that rots in the grave? Do you think I do not pity her cold blighted love for me? I fought against her spirit while

she lived to the bitter end. [*He presses his hand to his forehead.*] It fights against me still—in here.

BEATRICE.
[*As before.*] O, do not speak like that.

RICHARD.
She drove me away. On account of her I lived years in exile and poverty too, or near it. I never accepted the doles she sent me through the bank. I waited, too, not for her death but for some understanding of me, her own son, her own flesh and blood; that never came.

BEATRICE.
Not even after Archie...?

RICHARD.
[*Rudely.*] My son, you think? A child of sin and shame! Are you serious? [*She raises her face and looks at him.*] There were tongues here ready to tell her all, to embitter her withering mind still more against me and Bertha and our godless nameless child. [*Holding out his hands to her.*] Can you not hear her mocking me while I speak? You must know the voice, surely, the voice that called you *the black protestant*, the pervert's daughter. [*With sudden selfcontrol.*] In any case a remarkable woman.

BEATRICE.
[*Weakly.*] At least you are free now.

RICHARD.
[*Nods.*] Yes, she could not alter the terms of my father's will nor live for ever.

BEATRICE.
[*With joined hands.*] They are both gone now, Mr Rowan. They both loved you, believe me. Their last thoughts were of you.

RICHARD.
[*Approaching, touches her lightly on the shoulder, and points to the crayon drawing on the wall.*] Do you see him there, smiling and handsome? His last thoughts! I remember the night he died. [*He pauses for an instant and then goes on calmly.*] I was a boy of fourteen. He called me to his bedside. He knew I wanted to go to the theatre to hear *Carmen*. He told my mother to give me a shilling. I kissed him and went. When I came home he was dead. Those were his last thoughts as far as I know.

BEATRICE.
The hardness of heart you prayed for... [*She breaks off.*]

RICHARD.
[*Unheeding.*] That is my last memory of him. Is there not something sweet and noble in it?

BEATRICE.
Mr Rowan, something is on your mind to make you speak like this. Something has changed you since you came back three months ago.

RICHARD.
[*Gazing again at the drawing, calmly, almost gaily.*] He will help me, perhaps, my smiling handsome father.

[*A knock is heard at the hall door on the left.*]

RICHARD.
[*Suddenly.*] No, no. Not the smiler, Miss Justice. The old mother. It is her spirit I need. I am going.

BEATRICE.
Someone knocked. They have come back.

RICHARD.
No, Bertha has a key. It is he. At least, I am going, whoever it is.

[*He goes out quickly on the left and comes back at once with his straw hat in his hand.*]

BEATRICE.
 He? Who?

RICHARD.
 O, probably Robert. I am going out through the garden. I cannot see him now. Say I have gone to the post. Goodbye.

BEATRICE.
 [*With growing alarm.*] It is Robert you do not wish to see?

RICHARD.
 [*Quietly.*] For the moment, yes. This talk has upset me. Ask him to wait.

BEATRICE.
 You will come back?

RICHARD.
 Please God.

[*He goes out quickly through the garden.* BEATRICE *makes as if to follow him and then stops after a few paces.* BRIGID *enters by the folding doors on the right and goes out on the left. The hall door is heard opening. A few seconds after* BRIGID *enters with* ROBERT HAND. ROBERT HAND *is a middlesized, rather stout man between thirty and forty. He is cleanshaven, with mobile features. His hair and eyes are dark and his complexion sallow. His gait and speech are rather slow. He wears a dark blue morning suit and carries in his hand a large bunch of red roses wrapped in tissue paper.*]

ROBERT.
 [*Coming towards her with outstretched hand which she*

takes.] My dearest coz! Brigid told me you were here. I had no notion. Did you send mother a telegram?

BEATRICE.

[*Gazing at the roses.*] No.

ROBERT.

[*Following her gaze.*] You are admiring my roses. I brought them to the mistress of the house. [*Critically.*] I am afraid they are not nice.

BRIGID.

O, they are lovely, sir. The mistress will be delighted with them.

ROBERT.

[*Lays the roses carelessly on a chair out of sight.*] Is nobody in?

BRIGID.

Yes, sir. Sit down, sir. They'll be here now any moment. The master was here.

[*She looks about her and with a half curtsey goes out on the right.*]

ROBERT.

[*After a short silence.*] How are you, Beatty? And how are all down in Youghal? As dull as ever?

BEATRICE.

They were well when I left.

ROBERT.

[*Politely.*] O, but I'm sorry I did not know you were coming. I would have met you at the train. Why did you do it? You have some queer ways about you, Beatty, haven't you?

BEATRICE.
[*In the same tone.*] Thank you, Robert. I am quite used to getting about alone.

ROBERT.
Yes, but I mean to say... O, well, you have arrived in your own characteristic way.

[*A noise is heard at the window and a boy's voice is heard calling, 'Mr Hand!'* ROBERT *turns.*]

By Jove, Archie, too, is arriving in a characteristic way!

[ARCHIE *scrambles into the room through the open window on the left and then rises to his feet, flushed and panting.* ARCHIE *is a boy of eight years, dressed in white breeches, jersey and cap. He wears spectacles, has a lively manner and speaks with the slight trace of a foreign accent.*]

BEATRICE.
[*Going towards him.*] Goodness gracious, Archie! What is the matter?

ARCHIE.
[*Rising, out of breath.*] Eh! I ran all the avenue.

ROBERT.
[*Smiles and holds out his hand.*] Good evening, Archie. Why did you run?

ARCHIE.
[*Shakes hands.*] Good evening. We saw you on the top of the tram, and I shouted *Mr Hand!* But you did not see me. But we saw you, mamma and I. She will be here in a minute. I ran.

BEATRICE.
[*Holding out her hand.*] And poor me!

ARCHIE.
[*Shakes hands somewhat shyly.*] Good evening, Miss Justice.

BEATRICE.
Were you disappointed that I did not come last Friday for the lesson?

ARCHIE.
[*Glancing at her, smiles.*] No.

BEATRICE.
Glad?

ARCHIE.
[*Suddenly.*] But today it is too late.

BEATRICE.
A very short lesson?

ARCHIE.
[*Pleased.*] Yes.

BEATRICE.
But now you must study, Archie.

ROBERT.
Were you at the bath?

ARCHIE.
Yes.

ROBERT.
Are you a good swimmer now?

ARCHIE.
[*Leans against the davenport.*] No. Mamma won't let me into the deep place. Can you swim well, Mr Hand?

ROBERT.
Splendidly. Like a stone.

ARCHIE.
[*Laughs.*] Like a stone! [*Pointing down.*] Down that way?

ROBERT.
[*Pointing.*] Yes, down; straight down. How do you say that over in Italy?

ARCHIE.
That? *Giù.* [*Pointing down and up.*] That is *giù* and this is *sù.* Do you want to speak to my pappie?

ROBERT.
Yes. I came to see him.

ARCHIE.
[*Going towards the study.*] I will tell him. He is in there, writing.

BEATRICE.
[*Calmly, looking at* ROBERT.] No; he is out. He is gone to the post with some letters.

ROBERT.
[*Lightly.*] O, never mind. I will wait if he is only gone to the post.

ARCHIE.
But mamma is coming. [*He glances towards the window.*] Here she is!

[ARCHIE *runs out by the door on the left.* BEATRICE *walks slowly towards the davenport.* ROBERT *remains standing. A short silence.* ARCHIE *and* BERTHA *come in through the door on the left.* BERTHA *is a young woman of graceful build. She has dark grey eyes, patient in expression, and soft features. Her manner is cordial and selfpossessed. She wears a lavender dress and carries her cream gloves knotted round the handle of her sunshade.*]

BERTHA.
[*Shaking hands.*] Good evening, Miss Justice. We thought you were still down in Youghal.

BEATRICE.
[*Shaking hands.*] Good evening, Mrs Rowan.

BERTHA.
[*Bows.*] Good evening, Mr Hand.

ROBERT.
[*Bowing.*] Good evening, *signora!* Just imagine, I didn't know either she was back till I found her here.

BERTHA.
[*To both.*] Did you not come together?

BEATRICE.
No. I came first. Mr Rowan was going out. He said you would be back any moment.

BERTHA.
I'm sorry. If you had written or sent over word by the girl this morning...

BEATRICE.
[*Laughs nervously.*] I arrived only an hour and a half ago. I thought of sending a telegram but it seemed too tragic.

BERTHA.
Ah? Only now you arrived?

ROBERT.
[*Extending his arms, blandly.*] I retire from public and private life. Her first cousin and a journalist, I know nothing of her movements.

BEATRICE.
[*Not directly to him.*] My movements are not very interesting.

ROBERT.
[*In the same tone.*] A lady's movements are always interesting.

BERTHA.
But sit down, won't you? You must be very tired.

BEATRICE.
[*Quickly.*] No, not at all. I just came for Archie's lesson.

BERTHA.
I wouldn't hear of such a thing, Miss Justice, after your long journey.

ARCHIE.
[*Suddenly to* BEATRICE.] And, besides, you didn't bring the music.

BEATRICE.
[*A little confused.*] That I forgot. But we have the old piece.

ROBERT.
[*Pinching* ARCHIE'S *ear.*] You little scamp. You want to get off the lesson.

BERTHA.
O, never mind the lesson. You must sit down and have a cup of tea now. [*Going towards the door on the right.*] I'll tell Brigid.

ARCHIE.
I will, mamma. [*He makes a movement to go.*]

BEATRICE.
No, please Mrs Rowan. Archie! I would really prefer...

ROBERT.
[*Quietly.*] I suggest a compromise. Let it be a half-lesson.

BERTHA.
But she must be exhausted.

BEATRICE.
[*Quickly.*] Not in the least. I was thinking of the lesson in the train.

ROBERT.
[*To* BERTHA.] You see what it is to have a conscience, Mrs Rowan.

ARCHIE.
Of my lesson, Miss Justice?

BEATRICE.
[*Simply.*] It is ten days since I heard the sound of a piano.

BERTHA.
O, very well. If that is it...

ROBERT.
[*Nervously, gaily.*] Let us have the piano by all means. I know what is in Beatty's ears at this moment. [*To* BEATRICE.] Shall I tell?

BEATRICE.
If you know.

ROBERT.
The buzz of the harmonium in her father's parlour. [*To* BEATRICE.] Confess.

BEATRICE.
[*Smiling.*] Yes. I can hear it.

ROBERT.
[*Grimly.*] So can I. The asthmatic voice of protestantism.

BERTHA.
Did you not enjoy yourself down there, Miss Justice?

ROBERT.
[*Intervenes.*] She did not, Mrs Rowan. She goes there on retreat, when the protestant strain in her prevails—gloom, seriousness, righteousness.

BEATRICE.
I go to see my father.

ROBERT.
[*Continuing.*] But she comes back here to my mother, you see. The piano influence is from our side of the house.

BERTHA.
[*Hesitating.*] Well, Miss Justice, if you would like to play something... But please don't fatigue yourself with Archie.

ROBERT.
[*Suavely.*] Do, Beatty. That is what you want.

BEATRICE.
If Archie will come?

ARCHIE.
[*With a shrug.*] To listen.

BEATRICE.
[*Takes his hand.*] And a little lesson, too. Very short.

BERTHA.
Well, afterwards you must stay to tea.

BEATRICE.
[*To* ARCHIE.] Come.

[BEATRICE *and* ARCHIE *go out together by the door on the left.* BERTHA *goes towards the davenport, takes off her hat and lays it with her sunshade on the desk. Then taking a key from a little flowervase, she opens a drawer of the davenport, takes out a slip of paper and closes the drawer again.* ROBERT *stands watching her.*]

BERTHA.
[*Coming towards him with the paper in her hand.*] You put this into my hand last night. What does it mean?

ROBERT.
Do you not know?

BERTHA.
[*Reads.*] *There is one word which I have never dared to say to you.* What is the word?

ROBERT.
That I have a deep liking for you.

[*A short pause. The piano is heard faintly from the upper room.*]

ROBERT.
[*Takes the bunch of roses from the chair.*] I brought these for you. Will you take them from me?

BERTHA.
[*Taking them.*] Thank you. [*She lays them on the table and unfolds the paper again.*] Why did you not dare to say it last night?

ROBERT.
I could not speak to you or follow you. There were too many people on the lawn. I wanted you to think over it and so I put it into your hand when you were going away.

BERTHA.
Now you have dared to say it.

ROBERT.
[*Moves his hand slowly past his eyes.*] You passed. The avenue was dim with dusky light. I could see the dark green masses of the trees. And you passed beyond them. You were like the moon.

BERTHA.
[*Laughs.*] Why like the moon?

ROBERT.
In that dress, with your slim body, walking with little even steps. I saw the moon passing in the dusk till you passed and left my sight.

BERTHA.
Did you think of me last night?

ROBERT.
[*Comes nearer.*] I think of you always—as something beautiful and distant—the moon or some deep music.

BERTHA.
[*Smiling.*] And last night which was I?

ROBERT.
I was awake half the night. I could hear your voice. I could see your face in the dark. Your eyes... I want to speak to you. Will you listen to me? May I speak?

BERTHA.
[*Sitting down.*] You may.

ROBERT.
[*Sitting beside her.*] Are you annoyed with me?

BERTHA.
No.

ROBERT.
I thought you were. You put away my poor flowers so quickly.

BERTHA.
[*Takes them from the table and holds them close to her face.*] Is this what you wish me to do with them?

ROBERT.
[*Watching her.*] Your face is a flower too—but more beautiful. A wild flower blowing in a hedge. [*Moving his chair closer to her.*] Why are you smiling? At my words?

BERTHA.
[*Laying the flowers in her lap.*] I am wondering if that is what you say—to the others.

ROBERT.
[*Surprised.*] What others?

BERTHA.
The other women. I hear you have so many admirers.

ROBERT.
[*Involuntarily.*] And that is why you too...?

BERTHA.
But you have, haven't you?

ROBERT.
Friends, yes.

BERTHA.
Do you speak to them in the same way?

ROBERT.
[*In an offended tone.*] How can you ask me such a question? What kind of person do you think I am? Or why do you listen to me? Did you not like me to speak to you in that way?

BERTHA.
What you said was very kind. [*She looks at him for a moment.*] Thank you for saying it—and thinking it.

ROBERT.
[*Leaning forward.*] Bertha!

BERTHA.
Yes?

ROBERT.
I have the right to call you by your name. From old times—nine years ago. We were Bertha—and Robert—then. Can we not be so now, too?

BERTHA.
[*Readily.*] O yes. Why should we not?

ROBERT.
Bertha, you knew. From the very night you landed on Kingstown pier. It all came back to me then. And you knew it. You saw it.

BERTHA.
No. Not that night.

ROBERT.
When?

BERTHA.
The night we landed I felt very tired and dirty. [*Shaking her head.*] I did not see it in you that night.

ROBERT.
[*Smiling.*] Tell me what did you see that night—your very first impression.

BERTHA.
[*Knitting her brows.*] You were standing with your back to the gangway, talking to two ladies.

ROBERT.
To two plain middleaged ladies, yes.

BERTHA.
I recognized you at once. And I saw that you had got fat.

ROBERT.
[*Takes her hand.*] And this poor fat Robert—do you dislike him then so much? Do you disbelieve all he says?

BERTHA.
I think men speak like that to all women whom they like or admire. What do you want me to believe?

ROBERT.
All men, Bertha?

BERTHA.
[*With sudden sadness.*] I think so.

ROBERT.
I too?

BERTHA.
Yes, Robert. I think you too.

ROBERT.
All then—without exception? Or with one exception? [*In a lower tone.*] Or is he too—Richard too—like us all—in that at least? Or different?

BERTHA.
[*Looks into his eyes.*] Different.

ROBERT.
Are you quite sure, Bertha?

BERTHA.
[*A little confused, tries to withdraw her hand.*] I have answered you.

ROBERT.
[*Suddenly.*] Bertha, may I kiss your hand? Let me. May I?

BERTHA.
If you wish.

[*He lifts her hand to his lips slowly. She rises suddenly and listens.*]

BERTHA.
Did you hear the garden gate?

ROBERT.
[*Rising also.*] No.

[*A short pause. The piano can be heard faintly from the upper room.*]

ROBERT.
[*Pleading.*] Do not go away. You must never go away now. Your life is here. I came for that too today—to speak to him—to urge him to accept this position. He must. And you must persuade him to. You have a great influence over him.

BERTHA.
You want him to remain here.

ROBERT.
Yes.

BERTHA.
Why?

ROBERT.
For your sake because you are unhappy so far away. For his sake too because he should think of his future.

BERTHA.
[*Laughing.*] Do you remember what he said when you spoke to him last night?

ROBERT.
About...? [*Reflecting.*] Yes. He quoted the *Our Father* about our daily bread. He said that to take care for the future is to destroy hope and love in the world.

BERTHA.
Do you not think he is strange?

ROBERT.
In that, yes.

BERTHA.
A little—mad?

ROBERT.
[*Comes closer.*] No. He is not. Perhaps we are. Why, do you...?

BERTHA.
[*Laughs.*] I ask you because you are intelligent.

ROBERT.
You must not go away. I will not let you.

BERTHA.
[*Looks full at him.*] You?

ROBERT.
Those eyes must not go away. [*He takes her hands.*] May I kiss your eyes?

BERTHA.
Do so.

[*He kisses her eyes and then passes his hand over her hair.*]

ROBERT.
Little Bertha!

BERTHA.
[*Smiling.*] But I am not so little. Why do you call me little?

ROBERT.
Little Bertha! One embrace? [*He puts his arm around her.*] Look into my eyes again.

BERTHA.
[*Looks.*] I can see the little gold spots. So many you have.

ROBERT.
[*Delighted.*] Your voice! Give me a kiss, a kiss with your mouth.

BERTHA.
Take it.

ROBERT.
I am afraid. [*He kisses her mouth and passes his hand many times over her hair.*] At last I hold you in my arms!

BERTHA.
And are you satisfied?

ROBERT.
Let me feel your lips touch mine.

BERTHA.
And then you will be satisfied?

ROBERT.
[*Murmurs.*] Your lips, Bertha!

BERTHA.
[*Closes her eyes and kisses him quickly.*] There. [*Puts her hands on his shoulders.*] Why don't you say: thanks?

ROBERT.
[*Sighs.*] My life is finished—over.

BERTHA.
O, don't speak like that now, Robert.

ROBERT.
Over, over. I want to end it and have done with it.

BERTHA.
[*Concerned but lightly.*] You silly fellow!

ROBERT.
[*Presses her to him.*] To end it all—death. To fall from a great high cliff, down, right down into the sea.

BERTHA.
Please, Robert...

ROBERT.
Listening to music and in the arms of the woman I love—the sea, music and death.

BERTHA.
[*Looks at him for a moment.*] The woman you love?

ROBERT.
[*Hurriedly.*] I want to speak to you, Bertha—alone—not here. Will you come?

BERTHA.
[*With downcast eyes.*] I too want to speak to you.

ROBERT.
[*Tenderly.*] Yes, dear, I know. [*He kisses her again.*] I will speak to you; tell you all; then. I will kiss you, then, long long kisses—when you come to me—long long sweet kisses.

BERTHA.
Where?

ROBERT.
[*In the tone of passion.*] Your eyes. Your lips. All your divine body.

BERTHA.
[*Repelling his embrace, confused.*] I meant where do you wish me to come.

ROBERT.
To my house. Not my mother's over there. I will write the address for you. Will you come?

BERTHA.
When?

ROBERT.
Tonight. Between eight and nine. Come. I will wait for you tonight. And every night. You will?

[*He kisses her with passion, holding her head between his hands. After a few instants she breaks from him. He sits down.*]

BERTHA.
[*Listening.*] The gate opened.

ROBERT.
[*Intensely.*] I will wait for you.

[*He takes the slip from the table.* BERTHA *moves away from him slowly.* RICHARD *comes in from the garden.*]

RICHARD.
[*Advancing, takes off his hat.*] Good afternoon.

ROBERT.
[*Rises, with nervous friendliness.*] Good afternoon, Richard.

BERTHA.
[*At the table, taking the roses.*] Look what lovely roses Mr Hand brought me.

ROBERT.
I am afraid they are overblown.

RICHARD.
[*Suddenly.*] Excuse me for a moment, will you?

[*He turns and goes into his study quickly.* ROBERT *takes a pencil from his pocket and writes a few words on the slip; then hands it quickly to* BERTHA.]

ROBERT.
[*Rapidly.*] The address. Take the tram at Lansdowne Road and ask to be let down near there.

BERTHA.
[*Takes it.*] I promise nothing.

ROBERT.
I will wait.

[RICHARD *comes back from the study.*]

BERTHA.
[*Going.*] I must put these roses in water.

RICHARD.
[*Handing her his hat.*] Yes, do. And please put my hat on the rack.

BERTHA.
[*Takes it.*] So I will leave you to yourselves for your talk. [*Looking round.*] Do you want anything? Cigarettes?

RICHARD.
Thanks. We have them here.

BERTHA.
Then I can go?

[*She goes out on the left with* RICHARD'S *hat, which she leaves in the hall, and returns at once; she stops for a moment at the davenport, replaces the slip in the drawer, locks it, and replaces the key, and, taking the roses, goes towards the right.* ROBERT *precedes her to open the door for her. She bows and goes out.*]

RICHARD.
[*Points to the chair near the little table on the right.*] Your place of honour.

ROBERT.
[*Sits down.*] Thanks. [*Passing his hand over his brow.*] Good Lord, how warm it is today! The heat pains me here in the eye. The glare.

RICHARD.
The room is rather dark, I think, with the blind down but if you wish...

ROBERT.
[*Quickly.*] Not at all. I know what it is—the result of night work.

RICHARD.
[*Sits on the lounge.*] Must you?

ROBERT.
[*Sighs.*] Eh, yes. I must see part of the paper through every night. And then my leading articles. We are approaching a difficult moment. And not only here.

RICHARD.
[*After a slight pause.*] Have you any news?

ROBERT.
[*In a different voice.*] Yes. I want to speak to you seriously. Today may be an important day for you—or rather, tonight. I saw the vicechancellor this morning.

He has the highest opinion of you, Richard. He has read your book, he said.

RICHARD.
Did he buy it or borrow it?

ROBERT.
Bought it, I hope.

RICHARD.
I shall smoke a cigarette. Thirtyseven copies have now been sold in Dublin.

[*He takes a cigarette from the box on the table, and lights it.*]

ROBERT.
[*Suavely, hopelessly.*] Well, the matter is closed for the present. You have your iron mask on today.

RICHARD.
[*Smoking.*] Let me hear the rest.

ROBERT.
[*Again seriously.*] Richard, you are too suspicious. It is a defect in you. He assured me he has the highest possible opinion of you, as everyone has. You are the man for the post, he says. In fact, he told me that, if your name goes forward, he will work might and main for you with the senate and I... will do my part, of course, in the press and privately. I regard it as a public duty. The chair of romance literature is yours by right, as a scholar, as a literary personality.

RICHARD.
The conditions?

ROBERT.
Conditions? You mean about the future?

RICHARD.
I mean about the past.

ROBERT.
[*Easily.*] That episode in your past is forgotten. An act of impulse. We are all impulsive.

RICHARD.
[*Looks fixedly at him.*] You called it an act of folly, then—nine years ago. You told me I was hanging a weight about my neck.

ROBERT.
I was wrong. [*Suavely.*] Here is how the matter stands, Richard. Everyone knows that you ran away years ago with a young girl... How shall I put it?... with a young girl not exactly your equal. [*Kindly.*] Excuse me, Richard, that is not my opinion nor my language. I am simply using the language of people whose opinions I don't share.

RICHARD.
Writing one of your leading articles, in fact.

ROBERT.
Put it so. Well, it made a great sensation at the time. A mysterious disappearance. My name was involved too, as best man, let us say, on that famous occasion. Of course, they think I acted from a mistaken sense of friendship. Well, all that is known. [*With some hesitation.*] But what happened afterwards is not known.

RICHARD.
No?

ROBERT.
Of course, it is your affair, Richard. However, you are

not so young now as you were then. The expression is quite in the style of my leading articles, isn't it?

RICHARD.

Do you, or do you not, want me to give the lie to my past life?

ROBERT.

I am thinking of your future life—here. I understand your pride and your sense of liberty. I understand their point of view also. However, there is a way out; it is simply this. Refrain from contradicting any rumours you may hear concerning what happened... or did not happen after you went away. Leave the rest to me.

RICHARD.

You will set these rumours afloat?

ROBERT.

I will. God help me.

RICHARD.

[*Observing him.*] For the sake of social conventions?

ROBERT.

For the sake of something else too—our friendship, our lifelong friendship.

RICHARD.

Thanks.

ROBERT.

[*Slightly wounded.*] And I will tell you the whole truth.

RICHARD.

[*Smiles and bows.*] Yes. Do, please.

ROBERT.

Not only for your sake. Also for the sake of—your present partner in life.

RICHARD.
I see.

[*He crushes his cigarette softly on the ashtray and then leans forward, rubbing his hands slowly.*]

RICHARD.
Why for her sake?

ROBERT.
[*Also leans forward, quietly.*] Richard, have you been quite fair to her? It was her own free choice, you will say. But was she really free to choose? She was a mere girl. She accepted all that you proposed.

RICHARD.
[*Smiles.*] That is your way of saying that she proposed what I would not accept.

ROBERT.
[*Nods.*] I remember. And she went away with you. But was it of her own free choice? Answer me frankly.

RICHARD.
[*Turns to him, calmly.*] I played for her against all that you say or can say; and I won.

ROBERT.
[*Nodding again.*] Yes, you won.

RICHARD.
[*Rises.*] Excuse me for forgetting. Will you have some whisky?

ROBERT.
All things come to those who wait.

[RICHARD *goes to the sideboard and brings a small tray with the decanter and glasses to the table where he sets it down.*]

RICHARD.
[*Sits down again, leaning back on the lounge.*] Will you please help yourself?

ROBERT.
[*Does so.*] And you? Steadfast? [RICHARD *shakes his head.*] Lord, when I think of our wild nights long ago— talks by the hour, plans, carouses, revelry...

RICHARD.
In our house.

ROBERT.
It is mine now. I have kept it ever since though I don't go there often. Whenever you like to come let me know. You must come some night. It will be old times again. [*He lifts his glass and drinks.*] Prosit!

RICHARD.
It was not only a house of revelry; it was to be the hearth of a new life. [*Musing.*] And in that name all our sins were committed.

ROBERT.
Sins! Drinking and blasphemy [*he points*] by me. And drinking and heresy, much worse [*he points again*] by you—are those the sins you mean?

RICHARD.
And some others.

ROBERT.
[*Lightly, uneasily.*] You mean the women. I have no remorse of conscience. Maybe you have. We had two keys on those occasions. [*Maliciously.*] Have you?

RICHARD.
[*Irritated.*] For you it was all quite natural?

ROBERT.
For me it is quite natural to kiss a woman whom I like. Why not? She is beautiful for me.

RICHARD.
[*Toying with the lounge cushion.*] Do you kiss everything that is beautiful for you?

ROBERT.
Everything—if it can be kissed. [*He takes up a flat stone which lies on the table.*] This stone, for instance. It is so cool, so polished, so delicate, like a woman's temple. It is silent, it suffers our passion; and it is beautiful. [*He places it against his lips.*] And so I kiss it because it is beautiful. And what is a woman? A work of nature, too, like a stone or a flower or a bird. A kiss is an act of homage.

RICHARD.
It is an act of union between man and woman. Even if we are often led to desire through the sense of beauty can you say that the beautiful is what we desire?

ROBERT.
[*Pressing the stone to his forehead.*] You will give me a headache if you make me think today. I cannot think today. I feel too natural, too common. After all, what is most attractive in even the most beautiful woman?

RICHARD.
What?

ROBERT.
Not those qualities which she has and other women have not but the qualities which she has in common with them. I mean... the commonest. [*Turning over the stone, he presses the other side to his forehead.*] I mean how her body develops heat when it is pressed, the

movement of her blood, how quickly she changes by digestion what she eats into—what shall be nameless. [*Laughing.*] I am very common today. Perhaps that idea never struck you?

RICHARD.
[*Drily.*] Many ideas strike a man who has lived nine years with a woman.

ROBERT.
Yes. I suppose they do.... This beautiful cool stone does me good. Is it a paperweight or a cure for headache?

RICHARD.
Bertha brought it home one day from the strand. She, too, says that it is beautiful.

ROBERT.
[*Lays down the stone quietly.*] She is right.

[*He raises his glass and drinks. A pause.*]

RICHARD.
Is that all you wanted to say to me?

ROBERT.
[*Quickly.*] There is something else. The vicechancellor sends you, through me, an invitation for tonight—to dinner at his house. You know where he lives? [RICHARD *nods.*] I thought you might have forgotten. Strictly private, of course. He wants to meet you again and sends you a very warm invitation.

RICHARD.
For what hour?

ROBERT.
Eight. But, like yourself, he is free and easy about time. Now, Richard, you must go there. That is all. I feel tonight will be the turningpoint in your life. You will live

here and work here and think here and be honoured here—among our people.

RICHARD.

[*Smiling.*] I can almost see two envoys starting for the United States to collect funds for my statue a hundred years hence.

ROBERT.

[*Agreeably.*] Once I made a little epigram about statues. All statues are of two kinds. [*He folds his arms across his chest.*] The statue which says: *How shall I get down?* and the other kind [*he unfolds his arms and extends his right arm, averting his head*] the statue which says: *In my time the dunghill was so high.*

RICHARD.

The second one for me, please.

ROBERT.

[*Lazily.*] Will you give me one of those long cigars of yours?

[RICHARD *selects a Virginia cigar from the box on the table and hands it to him with the straw drawn out.*]

ROBERT.

[*Lighting it.*] These cigars Europeanize me. If Ireland is to become a new Ireland she must first become European. And that is what you are here for, Richard. Some day we shall have to choose between England and Europe. I am a descendant of the dark foreigners: that is why I like to be here. I may be childish. But where else in Dublin can I get a bandit cigar like this or a cup of black coffee? The man who drinks black coffee is going to conquer Ireland. And now I will take just a half measure of that whisky, Richard, to show you there is no ill feeling.

RICHARD.
[*Points.*] Help yourself.

ROBERT.
[*Does so.*] Thanks. [*He drinks and goes on as before.*] Then you yourself, the way you loll on that lounge: then your boy's voice and also—Bertha herself. Do you allow me to call her that, Richard? I mean as an old friend of both of you.

RICHARD.
O why not?

ROBERT.
[*With animation.*] You have that fierce indignation which lacerated the heart of Swift. You have fallen from a higher world, Richard, and you are filled with fierce indignation, when you find that life is cowardly and ignoble. While I... shall I tell you?

RICHARD.
By all means.

ROBERT.
[*Archly.*] I have come up from a lower world and I am filled with astonishment when I find that people have any redeeming virtue at all.

RICHARD.
[*Sits up suddenly and leans his elbows on the table.*] You are my friend, then?

ROBERT.
[*Gravely.*] I fought for you all the time you were away. I fought to bring you back. I fought to keep your place for you here. I will fight for you still because I have faith in you, the faith of a disciple in his master. I cannot say more than that. It may seem strange to you... Give me a match.

RICHARD.
[*Lights and offers him a match.*] There is a faith still stranger than the faith of the disciple in his master.

ROBERT.
And that is?

RICHARD.
The faith of a master in the disciple who will betray him.

ROBERT.
The church lost a theologian in you, Richard. But I think you look too deeply into life. [*He rises, pressing* RICHARD'S *arm slightly.*] Be gay. Life is not worth it.

RICHARD.
[*Without rising.*] Are you going?

ROBERT.
Must. [*He turns and says in a friendly tone.*] Then it is all arranged. We meet tonight at the vicechancellor's. I shall look in at about ten. So you can have an hour or so to yourselves first. You will wait till I come?

RICHARD.
Good.

ROBERT.
One more match and I am happy.

[RICHARD *strikes another match, hands it to him and rises also.* ARCHIE *comes in by the door on the left, followed by* BEATRICE.]

ROBERT.
Congratulate me, Beatty. I have won over Richard.

ARCHIE.
[*Crossing to the door on the right, calls.*] Mamma, Miss Justice is going.

BEATRICE.
On what are you to be congratulated?

ROBERT.
On a victory, of course. [*Laying his hand lightly on* RICHARD'S *shoulder.*] The descendant of Archibald Hamilton Rowan has come home.

RICHARD.
I am not a descendant of Hamilton Rowan.

ROBERT.
What matter?

[BERTHA *comes in from the right with a bowl of roses.*]

BEATRICE.
Has Mr Rowan...?

ROBERT.
[*Turning towards* BERTHA.] Richard is coming tonight to the vicechancellor's dinner. The fatted calf will be eaten: roast, I hope. And next session will see the descendant of a namesake of etcetera, etcetera in a chair of the university. [*He offers his hand.*] Good afternoon, Richard. We shall meet tonight.

RICHARD.
[*Touches his hand.*] At Philippi.

BEATRICE.
[*Shakes hands also.*] Accept my best wishes, Mr Rowan.

RICHARD.
Thanks. But do not believe him.

ROBERT.
[*Vivaciously.*] Believe me, believe me. [*To* BERTHA.] Good afternoon, Mrs Rowan.

BERTHA.
[*Shaking hands, candidly.*] I thank you, too. [*To* BEATRICE.] You won't stay to tea, Miss Justice?

BEATRICE.
No, thank you. [*Takes leave of her.*] I must go. Good afternoon. Goodbye, Archie [*going*].

ROBERT.
Addio, Archibald.

ARCHIE.
Addio.

ROBERT.
Wait, Beatty. I shall accompany you.

BEATRICE.
[*Going out on the right with* BERTHA.] O, don't trouble.

ROBERT.
[*Following her.*] But I insist—as a cousin.

[BERTHA, BEATRICE *and* ROBERT *go out by the door on the left.* RICHARD *stands irresolutely near the table.* ARCHIE *closes the door leading to the hall and, coming over to him, plucks him by the sleeve.*]

ARCHIE.
I say, pappie!

RICHARD.
[*Absently.*] What is it?

ARCHIE.
I want to ask you a thing.

RICHARD.
[*Sitting on the end of the lounge, stares in front of him.*]
What is it?

ARCHIE.
Will you ask mamma to let me go out in the morning with the milkman?

RICHARD.
With the milkman?

ARCHIE.
Yes. In the milkcar. He says he will let me drive when we get on to the roads where there are no people. The horse is a very good beast. Can I go?

RICHARD.
Yes.

ARCHIE.
Ask mamma now can I go. Will you?

RICHARD.
[*Glances towards the door.*] I will.

ARCHIE.
He said he will show me the cows he has in the field. Do you know how many cows he has?

RICHARD.
How many?

ARCHIE.
Eleven. Eight red and three white. But one is sick now. No, not sick. But it fell.

RICHARD.
Cows?

ARCHIE.
[*With a gesture.*] Eh! Not bulls. Because bulls give no

milk. Eleven cows. They must give a lot of milk. What makes a cow give milk?

RICHARD.

[*Takes his hand.*] Who knows? Do you understand what it is to give a thing?

ARCHIE.

To give? Yes.

RICHARD.

While you have a thing it can be taken from you.

ARCHIE.

By robbers? No?

RICHARD.

But when you give it, you have given it. No robber can take it from you. [*He bends his head and presses his son's hand against his cheek.*] It is yours then for ever when you have given it. It will be yours always. That is to give.

ARCHIE.

But, pappie?

RICHARD.

Yes?

ARCHIE.

How could a robber rob a cow? Everyone would see him. In the night, perhaps.

RICHARD.

In the night, yes.

ARCHIE.

Are there robbers here like in Rome?

RICHARD.

There are poor people everywhere.

ARCHIE.
Have they revolvers?

RICHARD.
No.

ARCHIE.
Knives? Have they knives?

RICHARD.
[*Sternly.*] Yes, yes. Knives and revolvers.

ARCHIE.
[*Disengages himself.*] Ask mamma now. She is coming.

RICHARD.
[*Makes a movement to rise.*] I will.

ARCHIE.
No, sit there, pappie. You wait and ask her when she comes back. I won't be here. I'll be in the garden.

RICHARD.
[*Sinking back again.*] Yes. Go.

ARCHIE.
[*Kisses him swiftly.*] Thanks.

[*He runs out quickly by the door at the back leading into the garden.* BERTHA *enters by the door on the left. She approaches the table and stands beside it, fingering the petals of the roses, looking at* RICHARD.]

RICHARD.
[*Watching her.*] Well?

BERTHA.
[*Absently.*] Well. He says he likes me.

RICHARD.
[*Leans his chin in his hand.*] You showed him his note?

BERTHA.
Yes. I asked him what it meant.

RICHARD.
What did he say it meant?

BERTHA.
He said I must know. I said I had an idea. Then he told me he liked me very much. That I was beautiful—and all that.

RICHARD.
Since when!

BERTHA.
[*Again absently.*] Since when—what?

RICHARD.
Since when did he say he liked you?

BERTHA.
Always, he said. But more since we came back. He said I was like the moon in this lavender dress. [*Looking at him.*] Had you any words with him—about me?

RICHARD.
[*Blandly.*] The usual thing. Not about you.

BERTHA.
He was very nervous. You saw that?

RICHARD.
Yes. I saw it. What else went on?

BERTHA.
He asked me to give him my hand.

RICHARD.
[*Smiling.*] In marriage?

BERTHA.
[*Smiling.*] No, only to hold.

RICHARD.
 Did you?

BERTHA.
 Yes. [*Tearing off a few petals.*] Then he caressed my hand and asked would I let him kiss it. I let him.

RICHARD.
 Well?

BERTHA.
 Then he asked could he embrace me—even once?... And then...

RICHARD.
And then?

BERTHA.
He put his arm round me.

RICHARD.
[*Stares at the floor for a moment, then looks at her again.*] And then?

BERTHA.
He said I had beautiful eyes. And asked could he kiss them. [*With a gesture.*] I said: *Do so.*

RICHARD.
And he did?

BERTHA.
Yes. First one and then the other. [*She breaks off suddenly.*] Tell me, Dick, does all this disturb you? Because I told you I don't want that. I think you are only pretending you don't mind. I don't mind.

RICHARD.
[*Quietly.*] I know, dear. But I want to find out what he means or feels just as you do.

BERTHA.
[*Points at him.*] Remember, you allowed me to go on. I told you the whole thing from the beginning.

RICHARD.
[*As before.*] I know, dear... And then?

BERTHA.
He asked for a kiss. I said: *Take it.*

RICHARD.
And then?

BERTHA.
[Crumpling a handful of petals.] He kissed me.

RICHARD.
Your mouth?

BERTHA.
Once or twice.

RICHARD.
Long kisses?

BERTHA.
Fairly long. [Reflects.] Yes, the last time.

RICHARD.
[Rubs his hands slowly; then.] With his lips? Or... the other way?

BERTHA.
Yes, the last time.

RICHARD.
Did he ask you to kiss him?

BERTHA.
He did.

RICHARD.
Did you?

BERTHA.
[Hesitates, then looking straight at him.] I did. I kissed him.

RICHARD.
What way?

BERTHA.
[With a shrug.] O simply.

RICHARD.
Were you excited?

BERTHA.
Well, you can imagine. [*Frowning suddenly.*] Not much. He has not nice lips... Still I was excited, of course. But not like with you, Dick.

RICHARD.
Was he?

BERTHA.
Excited? Yes, I think he was. He sighed. He was dreadfully nervous.

RICHARD.
[*Resting his forehead on his hand.*] I see.

BERTHA.
[*Crosses towards the lounge and stands near him.*] Are you jealous?

RICHARD.
[*As before.*] No.

BERTHA.
[*Quietly.*] You are, Dick.

RICHARD.
I am not. Jealous of what?

BERTHA.
Because he kissed me.

RICHARD.
[*Looks up.*] Is that all?

BERTHA.
Yes, that's all. Except that he asked me would I meet him.

RICHARD.
Out somewhere?

BERTHA.
No. In his house.

RICHARD.
[*Surprised.*] Over there with his mother, is it?

BERTHA.
No, a house he has. He wrote the address for me.

[*She goes to the desk, takes the key from the flower vase, unlocks the drawer and returns to him with the slip of paper.*]

RICHARD.
[*Half to himself.*] Our cottage.

BERTHA.
[*Hands him the slip.*] Here.

RICHARD.
[*Reads it.*] Yes. Our cottage.

BERTHA.
Your...?

RICHARD.
No, his. I call it ours. [*Looking at her.*] The cottage I told you about so often—that we had the two keys for, he and I. It is his now. Where we used to hold our wild nights, talking, drinking, planning—at that time. Wild nights; yes. He and I together. [*He throws the slip on the couch and rises suddenly.*] And sometimes I alone. [*Stares at her.*] But not quite alone. I told you. You remember?

BERTHA.
[*Shocked.*] That place?

RICHARD.
[*Walks away from her a few paces and stands still, thinking, holding his chin.*] Yes.

BERTHA.
[*Taking up the slip again.*] Where is it?

RICHARD.
Do you not know?

BERTHA.
He told me to take the tram at Lansdowne Road and to ask the man to let me down there. Is it... is it a bad place?

RICHARD.
O no, cottages. [*He returns to the lounge and sits down.*] What answer did you give?

BERTHA.
No answer. He said he would wait.

RICHARD.
Tonight?

BERTHA.
Every night, he said. Between eight and nine.

RICHARD.
And so I am to go tonight to interview—the professor. About the appointment I am to beg for. [*Looking at her.*] The interview is arranged for tonight by him—between eight and nine. Curious, isn't it? The same hour.

BERTHA.
Very.

RICHARD.
Did he ask you had I any suspicion?

BERTHA.
No.

RICHARD.
Did he mention my name?

BERTHA.
No.

RICHARD.
Not once?

BERTHA.
Not that I remember.

RICHARD.
[*Bounding to his feet.*] O yes! Quite clear!

BERTHA.
What?

RICHARD.
[*Striding to and fro.*] A liar, a thief, and a fool! Quite clear! A common thief! What else? [*With a harsh laugh.*] My great friend! A patriot too! A thief—nothing else! [*He halts, thrusting his hands into his pockets.*] But a fool also!

BERTHA.
[*Looking at him.*] What are you going to do?

RICHARD.
[*Shortly.*] Follow him. Find him. Tell him. [*Calmly.*] A few words will do. Thief and fool.

BERTHA.
[*Flings the slip on the couch.*] I see it all!

RICHARD.
[*Turning.*] Eh!

BERTHA.
[*Hotly.*] The work of a devil.

RICHARD.
He?

BERTHA.
[*Turning on him.*] No, you! The work of a devil to turn him against me as you tried to turn my own child against me. Only you did not succeed.

RICHARD.
How? In God's name, how?

BERTHA.
[*Excitedly.*] Yes, yes. What I say. Everyone saw it. Whenever I tried to correct him for the least thing you went on with your folly, speaking to him as if he were a grownup man. Ruining the poor child, or trying to. Then, of course, I was the cruel mother and only you loved him. [*With growing excitement.*] But you did not turn him against me—against his own mother. Because why? Because the child has too much nature in him.

RICHARD.
I never tried to do such a thing, Bertha. You know I cannot be severe with a child.

BERTHA.
Because you never loved your own mother. A mother is always a mother, no matter what. I never heard of any human being that did not love the mother that brought him into the world, except you.

RICHARD.
[*Approaching her quietly.*] Bertha, do not say things you will be sorry for. Are you not glad my son is fond of me?

BERTHA.
Who taught him to be? Who taught him to run to meet you? Who told him you would bring him home toys when you were out on your rambles in the rain, forgetting all about him—and me? I did. I taught him to love you.

RICHARD.
Yes, dear. I know it was you.

BERTHA.
[*Almost crying.*] And then you try to turn everyone against me. All is to be for you. I am to appear false and cruel to everyone except to you. Because you take advantage of my simplicity as you did—the first time.

RICHARD.
[*Violently.*] And you have the courage to say that to me?

BERTHA.
[*Facing him.*] Yes, I have! Both then and now. Because I am simple you think you can do what you like with me. [*Gesticulating.*] Follow him now. Call him names. Make him be humble before you and make him despise me. Follow him!

RICHARD.
[*Controlling himself.*] You forget that I have allowed you complete liberty—and allow you it still.

BERTHA.
[*Scornfully.*] Liberty!

RICHARD.
Yes, complete. But he must know that I know. [*More calmly.*] I will speak to him quietly. [*Appealing.*] Bertha, believe me, dear! It is not jealousy. You have complete liberty to do as you wish—you and he. But not in this

way. He will not despise you. You don't wish to deceive me or to pretend to deceive me—with him, do you?

BERTHA.

No, I do not. [*Looking full at him.*] Which of us two is the deceiver?

RICHARD.

Of us? You and me?

BERTHA.

[*In a calm decided tone.*] I know why you have allowed me what you call complete liberty.

RICHARD.

Why?

BERTHA.

To have complete liberty with—that girl.

RICHARD.

[*Irritated.*] But, good God, you knew about that this long time. I never hid it.

BERTHA.

You did. I thought it was a kind of friendship between you—till we came back, and then I saw.

RICHARD.

So it is, Bertha.

BERTHA.

[*Shakes her head.*] No, no. It is much more; and that is why you give me complete liberty. All those things you sit up at night to write about [*pointing to the study*] in there—about her. You call that friendship?

RICHARD.

Believe me, Bertha dear. Believe me as I believe you.

BERTHA.
[*With an impulsive gesture.*] My God, I feel it! I know it! What else is between you but love?

RICHARD.
[*Calmly.*] You are trying to put that idea into my head but I warn you that I don't take my ideas from other people.

BERTHA.
[*Hotly.*] It is, it is! And that is why you allow him to go on. Of course! It doesn't affect you. You love her.

RICHARD.
Love! [*Throws out his hands with a sigh and moves away from her.*] I cannot argue with you.

BERTHA.
You can't because I am right. [*Following him a few steps.*] What would anyone say?

RICHARD.
[*Turns to her.*] Do you think I care?

BERTHA.
But I care. What would he say if he knew? You, who talk so much of the high kind of feeling you have for me, expressing yourself in that way to another woman. If he did it, or other men, I could understand because they are false pretenders. But you, Dick! Why do you not tell him then?

RICHARD.
You can if you like.

BERTHA.
I will. Certainly I will.

RICHARD.
[*Coolly.*] He will explain it to you.

BERTHA.
He doesn't say one thing and do another. He is honest in his own way.

RICHARD.
[*Plucks one of the roses and throws it at her feet.*] He is, indeed! The soul of honour!

BERTHA.
You may make fun of him as much as you like. I understand more than you think about that business. And so will he. Writing those long letters to her for years, and she to you. For years. But since I came back I understand it—well.

RICHARD.
You do not. Nor would he.

BERTHA.
[*Laughs scornfully.*] Of course. Neither he nor I can understand it. Only she can. Because it is such a deep thing!

RICHARD.
[*Angrily.*] Neither he nor you—nor she either! Not one of you!

BERTHA.
[*With great bitterness.*] She will! She will understand it! The diseased woman!

[*She turns away and walks over to the little table on the right.* RICHARD *restrains a sudden gesture. A short pause.*]

RICHARD.
[*Gravely.*] Bertha, take care of uttering words like that!

BERTHA.
[*Turning, excitedly.*] I don't mean any harm! I feel for

her more than you can because I am a woman. I do, sincerely. But what I say is true.

RICHARD.
Is it generous? Think.

BERTHA.
[*Pointing towards the garden.*] It is she who is not generous. Remember now what I say.

RICHARD.
What?

BERTHA.
[*Comes nearer; in a calmer tone.*] You have given that woman very much, Dick. And she may be worthy of it. And she may understand it all, too. I know she is that kind.

RICHARD.
Do you believe that?

BERTHA.
I do. But I believe you will get very little from her in return—or from any of her clan. Remember my words, Dick. Because she is not generous and they are not generous. Is it all wrong what I am saying? Is it?

RICHARD.
[*Darkly.*] No. Not all.

[*She stoops and, picking up the rose from the floor, places it in the vase again. He watches her.* BRIGID *appears at the folding doors on the right.*]

BRIGID.
The tea is on the table, ma'am.

BERTHA.
Very well.

BRIGID.
Is Master Archie in the garden?

BERTHA.
Yes. Call him in.

[BRIGID *crosses the room and goes out into the garden.* BERTHA *goes towards the doors on the right. At the lounge she stops and takes up the slip.*]

BRIGID.
[*In the garden.*] Master Archie! You are to come in to your tea.

BERTHA.
Am I to go to this place?

RICHARD.
Do you want to go?

BERTHA.
I want to find out what he means. Am I to go?

RICHARD.
Why do you ask me? Decide yourself.

BERTHA.
Do you tell me to go?

RICHARD.
No.

BERTHA.
Do you forbid me to go?

RICHARD.
No.

BRIGID.
[*From the garden.*] Come quickly, Master Archie! Your tea is waiting on you.

[BRIGID *crosses the room and goes out through the folding doors.* BERTHA *folds the slip into the waist of her dress and goes slowly towards the right. Near the door she turns and halts.*]

BERTHA.
 Tell me not to go and I will not.

RICHARD.
 [*Without looking at her.*] Decide yourself.

BERTHA.
 Will you blame me then?

RICHARD.
 [*Excitedly.*] No, no! I will not blame you. You are free. I cannot blame you.

[ARCHIE *appears at the garden door.*]

BERTHA.
 I did not deceive you.

[*She goes out through the folding doors.* RICHARD *remains standing at the table.* ARCHIE, *when his mother has gone, runs down to* RICHARD.]

ARCHIE.
 [*Quickly.*] Well, did you ask her?

RICHARD.
 [*Starting.*] What?

ARCHIE.
 Can I go?

RICHARD.
 Yes.

ARCHIE.
 In the morning? She said yes?

RICHARD.
Yes. In the morning.

[*He puts his arm round his son's shoulders and looks down at him fondly.*]

Second Act

A room in Robert Hand's cottage at Ranelagh. On the right, forward, a small black piano, on the rest of which is an open piece of music. Farther back a door leading to the street door. In the wall, at the back, folding doors, draped with dark curtains, leading to a bedroom. Near the piano a large table, on which is a tall oil lamp with a wide yellow shade. Chairs, upholstered, near this table. A small cardtable more forward. Against the back wall a bookcase. In the left wall, back, a window looking out into the garden, and, forward, a door and porch, also leading to the garden. Easychairs here and there. Plants in the porch and near the draped folding doors. On the walls are many framed black and white designs. In the right corner, back, a sideboard; and in the centre of the room, left of the table, a group consisting of a standing Turkish pipe, a low oil stove, which is not lit, and a rocking-chair. It is the evening of the same day.

[ROBERT HAND, *in evening dress, is seated at the piano. The candles are not lit but the lamp on the table is lit. He plays softly in the bass the first bars of Wolfram's song in the last act of 'Tannhäuser'. Then he breaks off and, resting an elbow on the ledge of the keyboard, meditates. Then he rises and, pulling out a pump from behind the piano, walks here and there in the room ejecting from it into the air sprays of perfume. He inhales the air slowly and then puts the pump back behind the piano. He sits down on a chair near the table and, smoothing his hair carefully, sighs once or twice. Then, thrusting his hands into his trousers pockets, he leans back, stretches out his legs, and waits. A knock is heard at the street door. He rises quickly.]*

ROBERT.
[*Exclaims.*] Bertha!

[*He hurries out by the door on the right. There is a noise of confused greeting. After a few moments* ROBERT *enters, followed by* RICHARD ROWAN, *who is in grey tweeds as before but holds in one hand a dark felt hat and in the other an umbrella.*]

ROBERT.
First of all let me put these outside.

[*He takes the hat and umbrella, leaves them in the hall and returns.*]

ROBERT.
[*Pulling round a chair.*] Here you are. You are lucky to find me in. Why didn't you tell me today? You were always a devil for surprises. I suppose my evocation of the past was too much for your wild blood. See how artistic I have become. [*He points to the walls.*] The piano is an addition since your time. I was just strumming out Wagner when you came. Killing time. You see I am ready for the fray. [*Laughs.*] I was just wondering how you and the vicechancellor were getting on together. [*With exaggerated alarm.*] But are you going in that suit? O well, it doesn't make much odds, I

suppose. But how goes the time? [*He takes out his watch.*] Twenty past eight already, I declare!

RICHARD.

 Have you an appointment?

ROBERT.

 [*Laughs nervously.*] Suspicious to the last!

RICHARD.

 Then I may sit down?

ROBERT.

 Of course, of course. [*They both sit down.*] For a few minutes, anyhow. Then we can both go on together. We are not bound for time. Between eight and nine, he said, didn't he? What time is it, I wonder? [*Is about to look again at his watch; then stops.*] Twenty past eight, yes.

RICHARD.

 [*Wearily, sadly.*] Your appointment also was for the same hour. Here.

ROBERT.

 What appointment?

RICHARD.

 With Bertha.

ROBERT.

 [*Stares at him.*] Are you mad?

RICHARD.

 Are you?

ROBERT.

 [*After a long pause.*] Who told you?

RICHARD.

 She.

[*A short silence.*]

ROBERT.
[*In a low voice.*] Yes. I must have been mad. [*Rapidly.*] Listen to me, Richard. It is a great relief to me that you have come—the greatest relief. I assure you that ever since this afternoon I have thought and thought how I could break it off without seeming a fool. A great relief! I even intended to send word... a letter, a few lines. [*Suddenly.*] But then it was too late... [*Passes his hand over his forehead.*] Let me speak frankly with you; let me tell you everything.

RICHARD.
I know everything. I have known for some time.

ROBERT.
Since when?

RICHARD.
Since it began between you and her.

ROBERT.
[*Again rapidly.*] Yes, I was mad. But it was merely lightheadedness. I admit that to have asked her here this evening was a mistake. I can explain everything to you. And I will. Truly.

RICHARD.
Explain to me what is the word you longed and never dared to say to her. If you can or will.

ROBERT.
[*Looks down, then raises his head.*] Yes. I will. I admire very much the personality of your... of... your wife. That is the word. I can say it. It is no secret.

RICHARD.
Then why did you wish to keep secret your wooing?

ROBERT.
Wooing?

RICHARD.
Your advances to her, little by little, day after day, looks, whispers. [*With a nervous movement of the hands.*] *Insomma*, wooing.

ROBERT.
[*Bewildered.*] But how do you know all this?

RICHARD.
She told me.

ROBERT.
This afternoon?

RICHARD.
No. Time after time, as it happened.

ROBERT.
You knew? From her? [RICHARD *nods.*]. You were watching us all the time?

RICHARD.
[*Very coldly.*] I was watching you.

ROBERT.
[*Quickly.*] I mean, watching me. And you never spoke! You had only to speak a word—to save me from myself. You were trying me. [*Passes his hand again over his forehead.*] It was a terrible trial: now also. [*Desperately.*] Well, it is past. It will be a lesson to me for all my life. You hate me now for what I have done and for...

RICHARD.
[*Quietly, looking at him.*] Have I said that I hate you?

ROBERT.
Do you not? You must.

RICHARD.
Even if Bertha had not told me I should have known. Did you not see that when I came in this afternoon I went into my study suddenly for a moment?

ROBERT.
You did. I remember.

RICHARD.
To give you time to recover yourself. It made me sad to see your eyes. And the roses too. I cannot say why. A great mass of overblown roses.

ROBERT.
I thought I had to give them. Was that strange? [*Looks at* RICHARD *with a tortured expression.*] Too many, perhaps? Or too old or common?

RICHARD.
That was why I did not hate you. The whole thing made me sad all at once.

ROBERT.
[*To himself.*] And this is real. It is happening—to us.

[*He stares before him for some moments in silence, as if dazed; then, without turning his head, continues.*]

ROBERT.
And she, too, was trying me; making an experiment with me for your sake!

RICHARD.
You know women better than I do. She says she felt pity for you.

ROBERT.
[*Brooding.*] Pitied me, because I am no longer... an ideal lover. Like my roses. Common, old.

RICHARD.
Like all men you have a foolish wandering heart.

ROBERT.
[*Slowly.*] Well, you spoke at last. You chose the right moment.

RICHARD.
[*Leans forward.*] Robert, not like this. For us two, no. Years, a whole life, of friendship. Think a moment. Since childhood, boyhood... No, no. Not in such a way—like thieves—at night. [*Glancing about him.*] And in such a place. No, Robert, that is not for people like us.

ROBERT.
What a lesson! Richard, I cannot tell you what a relief it is to me that you have spoken—that the danger is passed. Yes, yes. [*Somewhat diffidently.*] Because... there was some danger for you, too, if you think. Was there not?

RICHARD.
What danger?

ROBERT.
[*In the same tone.*] I don't know. I mean if you had not spoken. If you had watched and waited on until...

RICHARD.
Until?

ROBERT.
[*Bravely.*] Until I had come to like her more and more (because I can assure you it is only a lightheaded idea of mine), to like her deeply, to love her. Would you have spoken to me then as you have just now? [RICHARD *is silent.* ROBERT *goes on more boldly.*] It would have been different, would it not? For then it might have been too late while it is not too late now. What could I have said

then? I could have said only: You are my friend, my dear good friend. I am very sorry but I love her. [*With a sudden fervent gesture.*] I love her and I will take her from you, however I can, because I love her.

[*They look at each other for some moments in silence.*]

RICHARD.

[*Calmly.*] That is the language I have heard often and never believed in. Do you mean by stealth or by violence? Steal you could not in my house because the doors were open; nor take by violence if there were no resistance.

ROBERT.

You forget that the kingdom of heaven suffers violence: and the kingdom of heaven is like a woman.

RICHARD.

[*Smiling.*] Go on.

ROBERT.

[*Diffidently, but bravely.*] Do you think you have rights over her—over her heart?

RICHARD.

None.

ROBERT.

For what you have done for her? So much! You claim nothing?

RICHARD.

Nothing.

ROBERT.

[*After a pause strikes his forehead with his hand.*] What am I saying? Or what am I thinking? I wish you would upbraid me, curse me, hate me as I deserve. You love this woman. I remember all you told me long ago. She is yours, your work. [*Suddenly.*] And that is why I, too, was drawn to her. You are so strong that you attract me even through her.

RICHARD.
I am weak.

ROBERT.
[*With enthusiasm.*] You, Richard! You are the incarnation of strength.

RICHARD.
[*Holds out his hands.*] Feel those hands.

ROBERT.
[*Taking his hands.*] Yes. Mine are stronger. But I meant strength of another kind.

RICHARD.
[*Gloomily.*] I think you would try to take her by violence.

[*He withdraws his hands slowly.*]

ROBERT.
[*Rapidly.*] Those are moments of sheer madness when we feel an intense passion for a woman. We see nothing. We think of nothing. Only to possess her. Call it brutal, bestial, what you will.

RICHARD.
[*A little timidly.*] I am afraid that that longing to possess a woman is not love.

ROBERT.
[*Impatiently.*] No man ever yet lived on this earth who did not long to possess—I mean to possess in the flesh—the woman whom he loves. It is nature's law.

RICHARD.
[*Contemptuously.*] What is that to me? Did I vote it?

ROBERT.
But if you love... What else is it?

RICHARD.
[*Hesitatingly.*] To wish her well.

ROBERT.
[*Warmly.*] But the passion which burns us night and day to possess her. You feel it as I do. And it is not what you said now.

RICHARD.
Have you...? [*He stops for an instance.*] Have you the luminous certitude that yours is the brain in contact with which she must think and understand and that yours is the body in contact with which her body must feel? Have you this certitude in yourself?

ROBERT.
Have you?

RICHARD.
[*Moved.*] Once I had it, Robert: a certitude as luminous as that of my own existence—or an illusion as luminous.

ROBERT.
[*Cautiously.*] And now?

RICHARD.
If you had it and I could feel that you had it—even now...

ROBERT.
What would you do?

RICHARD.
[*Quietly.*] Go away. You, and not I, would be necessary to her. Alone as I was before I met her.

ROBERT.
[*Rubs his hands nervously.*] A nice little load on my conscience!

RICHARD.
[*Abstractedly.*] You met my son when you came to my house this afternoon. He told me. What did you feel?

ROBERT.
[*Promptly.*] Pleasure.

RICHARD.
Nothing else?

ROBERT.
Nothing else. Unless I thought of two things at the same time. I am like that. If my best friend lay in his coffin and his face had a comic expression I should smile. [*With a little gesture of despair.*] I am like that. But I should suffer too, deeply.

RICHARD.
You spoke of conscience... Did he seem to you a child only—or an angel?

ROBERT.
[*Shakes his head.*] No. Neither an angel nor an Anglo-Saxon. Two things, by the way, for which I have very little sympathy.

RICHARD.
Never then? Never even... with her? Tell me. I wish to know.

ROBERT.
I feel in my heart something different. I believe that on

the last day (if it ever comes), when we are all assembled together, that the Almighty will speak to us like this. We will say that we lived chastely with one other creature...

RICHARD.
[*Bitterly.*] Lie to Him?

ROBERT.
Or that we tried to. And He will say to us: Fools! Who told you that you were to give yourselves to one being only? You were made to give yourselves to many freely. I wrote that law with My finger on your hearts.

RICHARD.
On woman's heart, too?

ROBERT.
Yes. Can we close our heart against an affection which we feel deeply? Should we close it? Should she?

RICHARD.
We are speaking of bodily union.

ROBERT.
Affection between man and woman must come to that. We think too much of it because our minds are warped. For us today it is of no more consequence than any other form of contact—than a kiss.

RICHARD.
If it is of no consequence why are you dissatisfied till you reach that end? Why were you waiting here tonight?

ROBERT.
Passion tends to go as far as it can; but, you may believe me or not, I had not that in my mind—to reach that end.

RICHARD.
Reach it if you can. I will use no arm against you that the world puts in my hand. If the law which God's finger has written on our hearts is the law you say I too am God's creature.

[*He rises and paces to and fro some moments in silence. Then he goes towards the porch and leans against the jamb.* ROBERT *watches him.*]

ROBERT.
I always felt it. In myself and in others.

RICHARD.
[*Absently.*] Yes?

ROBERT.
[*With a vague gesture.*] For all. That a woman, too, has the right to try with many men until she finds love. An immoral idea, is it not? I wanted to write a book about it. I began it...

RICHARD.
[*As before.*] Yes?

ROBERT.
Because I knew a woman who seemed to me to be doing that—carrying out that idea in her own life. She interested me very much.

RICHARD.
When was this?

ROBERT.
O, not lately. When you were away.

[RICHARD *leaves his place rather abruptly and again paces to and fro.*]

ROBERT.
You see, I am more honest than you thought.

RICHARD.
I wish you had not thought of her now—whoever she was, or is.

ROBERT.
[*Easily.*] She was and is the wife of a stockbroker.

RICHARD.
[*Turning.*] You know him?

ROBERT.
Intimately.

[RICHARD *sits down again in the same place and leans forward, his head on his hands.*]

ROBERT.
[*Moving his chair a little closer.*] May I ask you a question?

RICHARD.
You may.

ROBERT.
[*With some hesitation.*] Has it never happened to you in these years—I mean when you were away from her, perhaps, or travelling—to... betray her with another. Betray her, I mean, not in love. Carnally, I mean... Has that never happened?

RICHARD.
It has.

ROBERT.
And what did you do?

RICHARD.
[*As before.*] I remember the first time. I came home. It

was night. My house was silent. My little son was sleeping in his cot. She, too, was asleep. I wakened her from sleep and told her. I cried beside her bed; and I pierced her heart.

ROBERT.
O, Richard, why did you do that?

RICHARD.
Betray her?

ROBERT.
No. But tell her, waken her from sleep to tell her. It was piercing her heart.

RICHARD.
She must know me as I am.

ROBERT.
But that is not you as you are. A moment of weakness.

RICHARD.
[*Lost in thought.*] And I was feeding the flame of her innocence with my guilt.

ROBERT.
[*Brusquely.*] O, don't talk of guilt and innocence. You have made her all that she is. A strange and wonderful personality—in my eyes, at least.

RICHARD.
[*Darkly.*] Or I have killed her.

ROBERT.
Killed her?

RICHARD.
The virginity of her soul.

ROBERT.
[*Impatiently.*] Well lost! What would she be without you?

RICHARD.
I tried to give her a new life.

ROBERT.
And you have. A new and rich life.

RICHARD.
Is it worth what I have taken from her—her girlhood, her laughter, her young beauty, the hopes in her young heart?

ROBERT.
[*Firmly.*] Yes. Well worth it. [*He looks at* RICHARD *for some moments in silence.*] If you had neglected her, lived wildly, brought her away so far only to make her suffer...

[*He stops.* RICHARD *raises his head and looks at him.*]

RICHARD.
If I had?

ROBERT.
[*Slightly confused.*] You know there were rumours here of your life abroad—a wild life. Some persons who knew you or met you or heard of you in Rome. Lying rumours.

RICHARD.
[*Coldly.*] Continue.

ROBERT.
[*Laughs a little harshly.*] Even I at times thought of her as a victim. [*Smoothly.*] And of course, Richard, I felt and knew all the time that you were a man of great talent—of something more than talent. And that was your excuse—a valid one in my eyes.

RICHARD.
Have you thought that it is perhaps now—at this moment—that I am neglecting her? [*He clasps his hands nervously and leans across toward* ROBERT.] I may be silent still. And she may yield to you at last—wholly and many times.

ROBERT.
[*Draws back at once.*] My dear Richard, my dear friend, I swear to you I could not make you suffer.

RICHARD.
[*Continuing.*] You may then know in soul and body, in a hundred forms, and ever restlessly, what some old theologian, Duns Scotus, I think, called a death of the spirit.

ROBERT.
[*Eagerly.*] A death. No; its affirmation! A death! The supreme instant of life from which all coming life proceeds, the eternal law of nature herself.

RICHARD.
And that other law of nature, as you call it: change. How will it be when you turn against her and against me; when her beauty, or what seems so to you now, wearies you and my affection for you seems false and odious?

ROBERT.
That will never be. Never.

RICHARD.
And you turn even against yourself for having known me or trafficked with us both?

ROBERT.
[*Gravely.*] It will never be like that, Richard. Be sure of that.

RICHARD.

[*Contemptuously.*] I care very little whether it is or not because there is something I fear much more.

ROBERT.

[*Shakes his head.*] You fear? I disbelieve you, Richard. Since we were boys together I have followed your mind. You do not know what moral fear is.

RICHARD.

[*Lays his hand on his arm.*] Listen. She is dead. She lies on my bed. I look at her body which I betrayed—grossly and many times. And loved, too, and wept over. And I know that her body was always my loyal slave. To me, to me only she gave... [*He breaks off and turns aside, unable to speak.*]

ROBERT.

[*Softly.*] Do not suffer, Richard. There is no need. She is loyal to you, body and soul. Why do you fear?

RICHARD.

[*Turns towards him, almost fiercely.*] Not that fear. But that I will reproach myself then for having taken all for myself because I would not suffer her to give to another what was hers and not mine to give, because I accepted from her her loyalty and made her life poorer in love. That is my fear. That I stand between her and any moments of life that should be hers, between her and you, between her and anyone, between her and anything. I will not do it. I cannot and I will not. I dare not.

[*He leans back in his chair breathless, with shining eyes.* ROBERT *rises quietly, and stands behind his chair.*]

ROBERT.
Look here, Richard. We have said all there is to be said. Let the past be past.

RICHARD.
[*Quickly and harshly.*] Wait. One thing more. For you, too, must know me as I am—now.

ROBERT.
More? Is there more?

RICHARD.
I told you that when I saw your eyes this afternoon I felt sad. Your humility and confusion, I felt, united you to me in brotherhood. [*He turns half round towards him.*] At that moment I felt our whole life together in the past, and I longed to put my arm around your neck.

ROBERT.
[*Deeply and suddenly touched.*] It is noble of you, Richard, to forgive me like this.

RICHARD.
[*Struggling with himself.*] I told you that I wished you not to do anything false and secret against me—against our friendship, against her; not to steal her from me craftly, secretly, meanly—in the dark, in the night— you, Robert, my friend.

ROBERT.
I know. And it was noble of you.

RICHARD.
[*Looks up at him with a steady gaze.*] No. Not noble. Ignoble.

ROBERT.
[*Makes an involuntary gesture.*] How? Why?

RICHARD.
[*Looks away again: in a lower voice.*] That is what I must tell you too. Because in the very core of my ignoble heart I longed to be betrayed by you and by her—in the dark, in the night—secretly, meanly, craftily. By you, my best friend, and by her. I longed for that passionately and ignobly, to be dishonoured for ever in love and in lust, to be...

ROBERT.
[*Bending down, places his hands over* RICHARD'S *mouth.*] Enough. Enough. [*He takes his hands away.*] But no. Go on.

RICHARD.
To be for ever a shameful creature and to build up my soul again out of the ruins of its shame.

ROBERT.
And that is why you wished that she...

RICHARD.
[*With calm.*] She has spoken always of her innocence, as I have spoken always of my guilt, humbling me.

ROBERT.
From pride, then?

RICHARD.
From pride and from ignoble longing. And from a motive deeper still.

ROBERT.
[*With decision.*] I understand you.

[*He returns to his place and begins to speak at once, drawing his chair closer.*]

ROBERT.
May it not be that we are here and now in the presence

of a moment which will free us both—me as well as you—from the last bonds of what is called morality. My friendship for you has laid bonds on me.

RICHARD.
Light bonds, apparently.

ROBERT.
I acted in the dark, secretly. I will do so no longer. Have you the courage to allow me to act freely?

RICHARD.
A duel—between us?

ROBERT.
[*With growing excitement.*] A battle of both our souls, different as they are, against all that is false in them and in the world. A battle of your soul against the spectre of fidelity, of mine against the spectre of friendship. All life is a conquest, the victory of human passion over the commandments of cowardice. Will you, Richard? Have you the courage? Even if it shatters to atoms the friendship between us, even if it breaks up for ever the last illusion in your own life? There was an eternity before we were born: another will come after we are dead. The blinding instant of passion alone—passion, free, unashamed, irresistible—that is the only gate by which we can escape from the misery of what slaves call life. Is not this the language of your own youth that I heard so often from you in this very place where we are sitting now? Have you changed?

RICHARD.
[*Passes his hand across his brow.*] Yes. It is the language of my youth.

ROBERT.
[*Eagerly, intensely.*] Richard, you have driven me up to

this point. She and I have only obeyed your will. You yourself have roused these words in my brain. Your own words. Shall we? Freely? Together?

RICHARD.

[*Mastering his emotion.*] Together no. Fight your part alone. I will not free you. Leave me to fight mine.

ROBERT.

[*Rises, decided.*] You allow me, then?

RICHARD.

[*Rises also, calmly.*] Free yourself.

[*A knock is heard at the hall door.*]

ROBERT.

[*In alarm.*] What does this mean?

RICHARD.

[*Calmly.*] Bertha, evidently. Did you not ask her to come?

ROBERT.

Yes, but... [*Looking about him.*] Then I am going, Richard.

RICHARD.

No. I am going.

ROBERT.

[*Desperately.*] Richard, I appeal to you. Let me go. It is over. She is yours. Keep her and forgive me, both of you.

RICHARD.

Because you are generous enough to allow me?

ROBERT.

[*Hotly.*] Richard, you will make me angry with you if you say that.

RICHARD.
Angry or not, I will not live on your generosity. You
have asked her to meet you here tonight and alone.
Solve the question between you.

ROBERT.
[*Promptly.*] Open the door. I shall wait in the garden.
[*He goes towards the porch.*] Explain to her, Richard, as
best you can. I cannot see her now.

RICHARD.
I shall go. I tell you. Wait out there if you wish.

[*He goes out by the door on the right.* ROBERT *goes out
hastily through the porch but comes back the same
instant.*]

ROBERT.
An umbrella! [*With a sudden gesture.*] O!

[*He goes out again through the porch. The hall door is
heard to open and close.* RICHARD *enters, followed by*
BERTHA, *who is dressed in a darkbrown costume and
wears a small dark red hat. She has neither umbrella nor
waterproof.*]

RICHARD.
[*Gaily.*] Welcome back to old Ireland!

BERTHA.
[*Nervously, seriously.*] Is this the place?

RICHARD.
Yes, it is. How did you find it?

BERTHA.
I told the cabman. I didn't like to ask my way. [*Looking
about her curiously.*] Was he not waiting? Has he gone
away?

RICHARD.
[*Points towards the garden.*] He is waiting. Out there. He was waiting when I came.

BERTHA.
[*Selfpossessed again.*] You see, you came after all.

RICHARD.
Did you think I would not?

BERTHA.
I knew you could not remain away. You see, after all you are like all other men. You had to come. You are jealous like the others.

RICHARD.
You seem annoyed to find me here.

BERTHA.
What happened between you?

RICHARD.
I told him I knew everything, that I had known for a long time. He asked how. I said from you.

BERTHA.
Does he hate me?

RICHARD.
I cannot read in his heart.

BERTHA.
[*Sits down helplessly.*] Yes. He hates me. He believes I made a fool of him—betrayed him. I knew he would.

RICHARD.
I told him you were sincere with him.

BERTHA.
He does not believe it. Nobody would believe it. I should have told him first—not you.

RICHARD.
I thought he was a common robber, prepared to use even violence against you. I had to protect you from that.

BERTHA.
That I could have done myself.

RICHARD.
Are you sure?

BERTHA.
It would have been enough to have told him that you knew I was here. Now I can find out nothing. He hates me. He is right to hate me. I have treated him badly, shamefully.

RICHARD.
[*Takes her hand.*] Bertha, look at me.

BERTHA.
[*Turns to him.*] Well?

RICHARD.
[*Gazes into her eyes and then lets her hand fall.*] I cannot read in your heart either.

BERTHA.
[*Still looking at him.*] You could not remain away. Do you not trust me? You can see I am quite calm. I could have hidden it all from you.

RICHARD.
I doubt that.

BERTHA.
[*With a slight toss of her head.*] O, easily if I had wanted to.

RICHARD.
[*Darkly.*] Perhaps you are sorry now that you did not.

BERTHA.
Perhaps I am.

RICHARD.
[*Unpleasantly.*] What a fool you were to tell me! It would have been so nice if you had kept it secret.

BERTHA.
As you do, no?

RICHARD.
As I do, yes. [*He turns to go.*] Goodbye for a while.

BERTHA.
[*Alarmed, rises.*] Are you going?

RICHARD.
Naturally. My part is ended here.

BERTHA.
To her, I suppose?

RICHARD.
[*Astonished.*] Who?

BERTHA.
Her ladyship. I suppose it is all planned so that you may have a good opportunity. To meet her and have an intellectual conversation!

RICHARD.
[*With an outburst of rude anger.*] To meet the devil's father!

BERTHA.
[*Unpins her hat and sits down.*] Very well. You can go. Now I know what to do.

RICHARD.
[*Returns, approaches her.*] You don't believe a word of what you say.

BERTHA.
[*Calmly.*] You can go. Why don't you?

RICHARD.
Then you have come here and led him on in this way on account of me. Is that how it is?

BERTHA.
There is one person in all this who is not a fool. And that is you. I am though. And he is.

RICHARD.
[*Continuing.*] If so you have indeed treated him badly and shamefully.

BERTHA.
[*Points at him.*] Yes. But it was your fault. And I will end it now. I am simply a tool for you. You have no respect for me. You never had because I did what I did.

RICHARD.
And has he respect?

BERTHA.
He has. Of all the persons I met since I came back he is the only one who has. And he knows what they only suspect. And that is why I liked him from the first and like him still. Great respect for me she has! Why did you not ask her to come away with you nine years ago?

RICHARD.
You know why, Bertha. Ask yourself.

BERTHA.
Yes, I know why. You knew the answer you would get. That is why.

RICHARD.
That is not why. I did not even ask you.

BERTHA.
Yes. You knew I would go, asked or not. I do things. But if I do one thing I can do two things. As I have the name I can have the gains.

RICHARD.
[*With increasing excitement.*] Bertha, I accept what is to be. I have trusted you. I will trust you still.

BERTHA.
To have that against me. To leave me then. [*Almost passionately.*] Why do you not defend me then against him? Why do you go away from me now without a word? Dick, my God, tell me what you wish me to do?

RICHARD.
I cannot, dear. [*Struggling with himself.*] Your own heart will tell you. [*He seizes both her hands.*] I have a wild delight in my soul, Bertha, as I look at you. I see you as you are yourself. That I came first in your life or before him then—that may be nothing to you. You may be his more than mine.

BERTHA.
I am not. Only I feel for him, too.

RICHARD.
And I do too. You may be his and mine. I will trust you, Bertha, and him too. I must. I cannot hate him since his arms have been around you. You have drawn us near together. There is something wiser than wisdom in your heart. Who am I that I should call myself master of your heart or of any woman's? Bertha, love him, be his, give yourself to him if you desire—or if you can.

BERTHA.
[*Dreamily.*] I will remain.

RICHARD.
Goodbye.

[*He lets her hand fall and goes out rapidly on the right. BERTHA remains sitting. Then she rises and goes timidly towards the porch. She stops near it and, after a little hesitation, calls into the garden.*]

BERTHA.
Is anyone out there?

[*At the same time she retreats towards the middle of the room. Then she calls again in the same way.*]

BERTHA.
Is anyone there?

[*ROBERT appears in the open doorway that leads in from the garden. His coat is buttoned and the collar is turned up. He holds the doorposts with his hands lightly and waits for BERTHA to see him.*]

BERTHA.
[*Catching sight of him, starts back: then, quickly.*] Robert!

ROBERT.
Are you alone?

BERTHA.
Yes.

ROBERT.
[*Looking towards the door on the right.*] Where is he?

BERTHA.
Gone. [*Nervously.*] You startled me. Where did you come from?

ROBERT.
[*With a movement of his head.*] Out there. Did he not tell you I was out there—waiting?

BERTHA.
[*Quickly.*] Yes, he told me. But I was afraid here alone. With the door open, waiting. [*She comes to the table and rests her hand on the corner.*] Why do you stand like that in the doorway?

ROBERT.
Why? I am afraid too.

BERTHA.
Of what?

ROBERT.
Of you.

BERTHA.
[*Looks down.*] Do you hate me now?

ROBERT.
I fear you. [*Clasping his hands at his back, quietly but a little defiantly.*] I fear a new torture—a new trap.

BERTHA.
[*As before.*] For what do you blame me?

ROBERT.
[*Comes forward a few steps, halts: then impulsively:*] Why did you lead me on? Day after day, more and more. Why did you not stop me? You could have—with a word. But not even a word! I forgot myself and him. You saw it. That I was ruining myself in his eyes, losing his friendship. Did you want me to?

BERTHA.
[*Looking up.*] You never asked me.

ROBERT.
 Asked you what?

BERTHA.
 If he suspected—or knew.

ROBERT.
 And would you have told me?

BERTHA.
 Yes.

ROBERT.
 [*Hesitatingly.*] Did you tell him—everything?

BERTHA.
 I did.

ROBERT.
 I mean—details.

BERTHA.
 Everything.

ROBERT.
 [*With a forced smile.*] I see. You were making an experiment for his sake. On me. Well, why not? It seems I was a good subject. Still, it was a little cruel of you.

BERTHA.
 Try to understand me, Robert. You must try.

ROBERT.
 [*With a polite gesture.*] Well, I will try.

BERTHA.
 Why do you stand like that near the door? It makes me nervous to look at you.

ROBERT.
 I am trying to understand. And then I am afraid.

BERTHA.
[*Holds out her hand.*] You need not be afraid.

[ROBERT *comes towards her quickly and takes her hand.*]

ROBERT.
[*Diffidently.*] Used you to laugh over me—together? [*Drawing his hand away.*] But now I must be good or you may laugh over me again—tonight.

BERTHA.
[*Distressed, lays her hand on his arm.*] Please listen to me, Robert... But you are all wet, drenched! [*She passes her hands over his coat.*] O, you poor fellow! Out there in the rain all that time! I forgot that.

ROBERT.
[*Laughs.*] Yes, you forgot the climate.

BERTHA.
But you are really drenched. You must change your coat.

ROBERT.
[*Takes her hands.*] Tell me, it is pity then that you feel for me, as he—as Richard—says?

BERTHA.
Please change your coat, Robert, when I ask you. You might get a very bad cold from that. Do, please.

ROBERT.
What would it matter now?

BERTHA.
[*Looking round her.*] Where do you keep your clothes here?

ROBERT.
[*Points to the door at the back.*] In there. I fancy I have a jacket here. [*Maliciously.*] In my bedroom.

BERTHA.
Well, go in and take that off.

ROBERT.
And you?

BERTHA.
I will wait here for you.

ROBERT.
Do you command me to?

BERTHA.
[*Laughing.*] Yes, I command you.

ROBERT.
[*Promptly.*] Then I will. [*He goes quickly towards the bedroom door; then turns round.*] You won't go away?

BERTHA.
No, I will wait. But don't be long.

ROBERT.
Only a moment.

[*He goes into the bedroom, leaving the door open.* BERTHA *looks curiously about her and then glances in indecision towards the door at the back.*]

ROBERT.
[*From the bedroom.*] You have not gone?

BERTHA.
No.

ROBERT.
I am in the dark here. I must light the lamp.

[*He is heard striking a match, and putting a glass shade on a lamp. A pink light comes in through the doorway.* BERTHA *glances at her watch at her wristlet and then sits at the table.*]

ROBERT.
 [*As before.*] Do you like the effect of the light?

BERTHA.
 O, yes.

ROBERT.
 Can you admire it from where you are?

BERTHA.
 Yes, quite well.

ROBERT.
 It was for you.

BERTHA.
 [*Confused.*] I am not worthy even of that.

ROBERT.
 [*Clearly, harshly.*] Love's labour lost.

BERTHA.
 [*Rising nervously.*] Robert!

ROBERT.
 Yes?

BERTHA.
 Come here, quickly! Quickly, I say!

ROBERT.
 I am ready.

[*He appears in the doorway, wearing a darkgreen velvet jacket. Seeing her agitation, he comes quickly towards her.*]

ROBERT.
What is it, Bertha?

BERTHA.
[*Trembling.*] I was afraid.

ROBERT.
Of being alone?

BERTHA.
[*Catches his hands.*] You know what I mean. My nerves are all upset.

ROBERT.
That I...?

BERTHA.
Promise me, Robert, not to think of such a thing. Never. If you like me at all. I thought that moment...

ROBERT.
What an idea?

BERTHA.
But promise me if you like me.

ROBERT.
If I like you, Bertha! I promise. Of course, I promise. You are trembling all over.

BERTHA.
Let me sit down somewhere. It will pass in a moment.

ROBERT.
My poor Bertha! Sit down. Come.

[*He leads her towards a chair near the table. She sits down. He stands beside her.*]

ROBERT.
[*After a short pause.*] Has it passed?

BERTHA.
Yes. It was only for a moment. I was very silly. I was afraid that... I wanted to see you near me.

ROBERT.
That... that you made me promise not to think of?

BERTHA.
Yes.

ROBERT.
[*Keenly.*] Or something else?

BERTHA.
[*Helplessly.*] Robert, I feared something. I am not sure what.

ROBERT.
And now?

BERTHA.
Now you are here. I can see you. Now it has passed.

ROBERT.
[*With resignation.*] Passed. Yes. Love's labour lost.

BERTHA.
[*Looks up at him.*] Listen, Robert. I want to explain to you about that. I could not deceive Dick. Never. In nothing. I told him everything—from the first. Then it went on and on; and still you never spoke or asked me. I wanted you to.

ROBERT.
Is that the truth, Bertha?

BERTHA.
Yes, because it annoyed me that you could think I was like... like the other women I suppose you knew that

way. I think that Dick is right too. Why should there be secrets?

ROBERT.
[*Softly.*] Still, secrets can be very sweet. Can they not?

BERTHA.
[*Smiles.*] Yes, I know they can. But, you see, I could not keep things secret from Dick. Besides, what is the good? They always come out in the end. Is it not better for people to know?

ROBERT.
[*Softly and a little shyly.*] How could you, Bertha, tell him everything? Did you? Every single thing that passed between us?

BERTHA.
Yes. Everything he asked me.

ROBERT.
Did he ask you—much?

BERTHA.
You know the kind he is. He asks about everything. The ins and outs.

ROBERT.
About our kissing, too?

BERTHA.
Of course. I told him all.

ROBERT.
[*Shakes his head slowly.*] Extraordinary little person! Were you not ashamed?

BERTHA.
No.

ROBERT.
Not a bit?

BERTHA.
No. Why? Is that terrible?

ROBERT.
And how did he take it? Tell me. I want to know everything, too.

BERTHA.
[*Laughs.*] It excited him. More than usual.

ROBERT.
Why? Is he excitable—still?

BERTHA.
[*Archly.*] Yes, very. When he is not lost in his philosophy.

ROBERT.
More than I?

BERTHA.
More than you? [*Reflecting.*] How could I answer that? You both are, I suppose?

[ROBERT *turns aside and gazes towards the porch, passing his hand once or twice thoughtfully over his hair.*]

BERTHA.
[*Gently.*] Are you angry with me again?

ROBERT.
[*Moodily.*] You are with me.

BERTHA.
No, Robert. Why should I be?

ROBERT.
Because I asked you to come to this place. I tried to

prepare it for you. [*He points vaguely here and there.*] A sense of quietness.

BERTHA.
[*Touching his jacket with her fingers.*] And this, too. Your nice velvet coat.

ROBERT.
Also. I will keep no secrets from you.

BERTHA.
You remind me of someone in a picture. I like you in it... But you are not angry, are you?

ROBERT.
[*Darkly.*] Yes. That was my mistake. To ask you to come here. I felt it when I looked at you from the garden and saw you—you, Bertha—standing here. [*Hopelessly.*] But what else could I have done?

BERTHA.
[*Quietly.*] You mean because others have been here?

ROBERT.
Yes.

[*He walks away from her a few paces. A gust of wind makes the lamp on the table flicker. He lowers the wick slightly.*]

BERTHA.
[*Following him with her eyes.*] But I knew that before I came. I am not angry with you for it.

ROBERT.
[*Shrugs his shoulders.*] Why should you be angry with me after all? You are not even angry with him—for the same thing—or worse.

BERTHA.
Did he tell you that about himself?

ROBERT.
Yes. He told me. We all confess to one another here. Turn about.

BERTHA.
I try to forget it.

ROBERT.
It does not trouble you?

BERTHA.
Not now. Only I dislike to think of it.

ROBERT.
It is merely something brutal, you think? Of little importance?

BERTHA.
It does not trouble me—now.

ROBERT.
[*Looking at her over his shoulder.*] But there is something that would trouble you very much and that you would not try to forget?

BERTHA.
What?

ROBERT.
[*Turning towards her.*] If it were not only something brutal with this person or that—for a few moments. If it were something fine and spiritual—with one person only—with one woman. [*Smiles.*] And perhaps brutal too. It usually comes to that sooner or later. Would you try to forget and forgive that?

BERTHA.
[*Toying with her wristlet.*] In whom?

ROBERT.
In anyone. In me.

BERTHA.
[*Calmly.*] You mean in Dick.

ROBERT.
I said in myself. But would you?

BERTHA.
You think I would revenge myself? Is Dick not to be free too?

ROBERT.
[*Points at her.*] That is not from your heart, Bertha.

BERTHA.
[*Proudly.*] Yes, it is; let him be free too. He leaves me free also.

ROBERT.
[*Insistently.*] And you know why? And understand? And you like it? And you want to be? And it makes you happy? And has made you happy? Always? This gift of freedom which he gave you—nine years ago?

BERTHA.
[*Gazing at him with wide open eyes.*] But why do you ask me such a lot of questions, Robert?

ROBERT.
[*Stretches out both hands to her.*] Because I had another gift to offer you then—a common simple gift—like myself. If you want to know it I will tell you.

BERTHA.
[*Looking at her watch.*] Past is past, Robert. And I think I ought to go now. It is nine almost.

ROBERT.
[*Impetuously.*] No, no. Not yet. There is one confession more and we have the right to speak.

[*He crosses before the table rapidly and sits down beside her.*]

BERTHA.
[*Turning towards him, places her left hand on his shoulder.*] Yes, Robert. I know that you like me. You need not tell me. [*Kindly.*] You need not confess any more tonight.

[*A gust of wind enters through the porch, with a sound of moving leaves. The lamp flickers quickly.*]

BERTHA.
[*Pointing over his shoulder.*] Look! It is too high.

[*Without rising, he bends towards the table, and turns down the wick more. The room is half dark. The light comes in more strongly through the doorway of the bedroom.*]

ROBERT.
The wind is rising. I will close that door.

BERTHA.
[*Listening.*] No, it is raining still. It was only a gust of wind.

ROBERT.
[*Touches her shoulder.*] Tell me if the air is too cold for you. [*Half rising.*] I will close it.

BERTHA.
[*Detaining him.*] No. I am not cold. Besides, I am going now, Robert. I must.

ROBERT.
[*Firmly.*] No, no. There is no *must* now. We were left here for this. And you are wrong, Bertha. The past is not past. It is present here now. My feeling for you is the same now as it was then, because then—you slighted it.

BERTHA.
No, Robert. I did not.

ROBERT.
[*Continuing.*] You did. And I have felt it all these years without knowing it—till now. Even while I lived—the kind of life you know and dislike to think of—the kind of life to which you condemned me.

BERTHA.
I?

ROBERT.

Yes, when you slighted the common simple gift I had to offer you—and took his gift instead.

BERTHA.

[*Looking at him.*] But you never...

ROBERT.

No. Because you had chosen him. I saw that. I saw it on the first night we met, we three together. Why did you choose him?

BERTHA.

[*Bends her head.*] Is that not love?

ROBERT.

[*Continuing.*] And every night when we two—he and I—came to that corner to meet you I saw it and felt it. You remember the corner, Bertha?

BERTHA.

[*As before.*] Yes.

ROBERT.

And when you and he went away for your walk and I went along the street alone I felt it. And when he spoke to me about you and told me he was going away—then most of all.

BERTHA.

Why then most of all?

ROBERT.

Because it was then that I was guilty of my first treason towards him.

BERTHA.

Robert, what are you saying? Your first treason against Dick?

ROBERT.
[*Nods.*] And not my last. He spoke of you and himself. Of how your life would be together—free and all that. Free, yes! He would not even ask you to go with him. [*Bitterly.*] He did not. And you went all the same.

BERTHA.
I wanted to be with him. You know... [*Raising her head and looking at him.*] You know how we were then—Dick and I.

ROBERT.
[*Unheeding.*] I advised him to go alone—not to take you with him—to live alone in order to see if what he felt for you was a passing thing which might ruin your happiness and his career.

BERTHA.
Well, Robert. It was unkind of you towards me. But I forgive you because you were thinking of his happiness and mine.

ROBERT.
[*Bending closer to her.*] No, Bertha. I was not. And that was my treason. I was thinking of myself—that you might turn from him when he had gone and he from you. Then I would have offered you my gift. You know what it was now. The simple common gift that men offer to women. Not the best perhaps. Best or worst—it would have been yours.

BERTHA.
[*Turning away from him.*] He did not take your advice.

ROBERT.
[*As before.*] No. And the night you ran away together— O, how happy I was!

BERTHA.
[*Pressing his hands.*] Keep calm, Robert. I know you liked me always. Why did you not forget me?

ROBERT.
[*Smiles bitterly.*] How happy I felt as I came back along the quays and saw in the distance the boat lit up going down the black river, taking you away from me! [*In a calmer tone.*] But why did you choose him? Did you not like me at all?

BERTHA.
Yes. I liked you because you were his friend. We often spoke about you. Often and often. Every time you wrote or sent papers or books to Dick. And I like you still, Robert. [*Looking into his eyes.*] I never forgot you.

ROBERT.
Nor I you. I knew I would see you again. I knew it the night you went away—that you would come back. And that was why I wrote and worked to see you again—here.

BERTHA.
And here I am. You were right.

ROBERT.
[*Slowly.*] Nine years. Nine times more beautiful!

BERTHA.
[*Smiling.*] But am I? What do you see in me?

ROBERT.
[*Gazing at her.*] A strange and beautiful lady.

BERTHA.
[*Almost disgusted.*] O, please don't call me such a thing!

ROBERT.
[*Earnestly.*] You are more. A young and beautiful queen.

BERTHA.
[*With a sudden laugh.*] O, Robert!

ROBERT.
[*Lowering his voice and bending nearer to her.*] But do you not know that you are a beautiful human being? Do you not know that you have a beautiful body? Beautiful and young?

BERTHA.
[*Gravely.*] Some day I will be old.

ROBERT.
[*Shakes his head.*] I cannot imagine it. Tonight you are young and beautiful. Tonight you have come back to me. [*With passion.*] Who knows what will be tomorrow? I may never see you again or never see you as I do now.

BERTHA.
Would you suffer?

ROBERT.
[*Looks round the room, without answering.*] This room and this hour were made for your coming. When you have gone—all is gone.

BERTHA.
[*Anxiously.*] But you will see me again, Robert... as before.

ROBERT.
[*Looks full at her.*] To make him—Richard—suffer.

BERTHA.
He does not suffer.

ROBERT.
[*Bowing his head.*] Yes, yes. He does.

BERTHA.
He knows we like each other. Is there any harm, then?

ROBERT.
[*Raising his head.*] No there is no harm. Why should we not? He does not know yet what I feel. He has left us alone here at night, at this hour, because he longs to know it—he longs to be delivered.

BERTHA.
From what?

ROBERT.
[*Moves closer to her and presses her arm as he speaks.*] From every law, Bertha, from every bond. All his life he has sought to deliver himself. Every chain but one he has broken and that one we are to break. Bertha—you and I.

BERTHA.
[*Almost inaudibly.*] Are you sure?

ROBERT.
[*Still more warmly.*] I am sure that no law made by man is sacred before the impulse of passion. [*Almost fiercely.*] Who made us for one only? It is a crime against our own being if we are so. There is no law before impulse. Laws are for slaves. Bertha, say my name! Let me hear your voice say it. Softly!

BERTHA.
[*Softly.*] Robert!

ROBERT.
[*Puts his arm about her shoulder.*] Only the impulse towards youth and beauty does not die. [*He points towards the porch.*] Listen!

BERTHA.
[*In alarm.*] What?

ROBERT.
The rain falling. Summer rain on the earth. Night rain. The darkness and warmth and flood of passion. Tonight the earth is loved—loved and possessed. Her lover's arms around her; and she is silent. Speak, dearest!

BERTHA.
[*Suddenly leans forward and listens intently.*] Hush!

ROBERT.
[*Listening, smiles.*] Nothing. Nobody. We are alone.

[*A gust of wind blows in through the porch, with a sound of shaken leaves. The flame of the lamp leaps.*]

BERTHA.
[*Pointing to the lamp.*] Look!

ROBERT.
Only the wind. We have light enough from the other room.

[*He stretches his hand across the table and puts out the lamp. The light from the doorway of the bedroom crosses the place where they sit. The room is quite dark.*]

ROBERT.
Are you happy? Tell me.

BERTHA.
I am going now, Robert. It is very late. Be satisfied.

ROBERT.
[*Caressing her hair.*] Not yet, not yet. Tell me, do you love me a little?

BERTHA.
I like you, Robert. I think you are good. [*Half rising.*] Are you satisfied?

ROBERT.
[*Detaining her, kisses her hair.*] Do not go, Bertha! There is time still. Do you love me too? I have waited a long time. Do you love us both—him and also me? Do you, Bertha? The truth! Tell me. Tell me with your eyes. Or speak!

[*She does not answer. In the silence the rain is heard falling.*]

Third Act

The drawingroom of Richard Rowan's house at Merrion. The folding doors at the right are closed and also the double doors leading to the garden. The green plush curtains are drawn across the window on the left. The room is half dark. It is early in the morning of the next day. Bertha sits beside the window looking out between the curtains. She wears a loose saffron dressing gown. Her hair is combed loosely over the ears and knotted at the neck. Her hands are folded in her lap. Her face is pale and drawn.

[Brigid *comes in through the folding doors on the right with a featherbroom and duster. She is about to cross but, seeing* Bertha, *she halts suddenly and blesses herself instinctively.*]

BRIGID.
Merciful hour, ma'am. You put the heart across me. Why did you get up so early?

BERTHA.
What time is it?

BRIGID.
After seven, ma'am. Are you long up?

BERTHA.
Some time.

BRIGID.
[*Approaching her.*] Had you a bad dream that woke you?

BERTHA.
I didn't sleep all night. So I got up to see the sun rise.

BRIGID.
[*Opens the double doors.*] It's a lovely morning now after all the rain we had. [*Turns round.*] But you must be dead tired, ma'am. What will the master say at your doing a thing like that? [*She goes to the door of the study and knocks.*] Master Richard!

BERTHA.
[*Looks round.*] He is not there. He went out an hour ago.

BRIGID.
Out there, on the strand, is it?

BERTHA.
Yes.

BRIGID.
[*Comes towards her and leans over the back of a chair.*] Are you fretting yourself, ma'am, about anything?

BERTHA.
No, Brigid.

BRIGID.
Don't be. He was always like that, meandering off by himself somewhere. He is a curious bird, Master Richard, and always was. Sure there isn't a turn in him I don't know. Are you fretting now maybe because he does be in there [*pointing to the study*] half the night at his books? Leave him alone. He'll come back to you again. Sure he thinks the sun shines out of your face, ma'am.

BERTHA.
[*Sadly.*] That time is gone.

BRIGID.
[*Confidentially.*] And good cause I have to remember it—that time when he was paying his addresses to you. [*She sits down beside* BERTHA. *In a lower voice.*] Do you know that he used to tell me all about you and nothing to his mother, God rest her soul? Your letters and all.

BERTHA.
What? My letters to him?

BRIGID.
[*Delighted.*] Yes. I can see him sitting on the kitchen table, swinging his legs and spinning out of him yards of talk about you and him and Ireland and all kinds of devilment—to an ignorant old woman like me. But that was always his way. But if he had to meet a grand highup person he'd be twice as grand himself. [*Suddenly looks at* BERTHA.] Is it crying you are now? Ah, sure, don't cry. There's good times coming still.

BERTHA.
No, Brigid, that time comes only once in a lifetime. The

rest of life is good for nothing except to remember that time.

BRIGID.
[*Is silent for a moment: then says kindly.*] Would you like a cup of tea, ma'am? That would make you all right.

BERTHA.
Yes, I would. But the milkman has not come yet.

BRIGID.
No. Master Archie told me to wake him before he came. He's going out for a jaunt in the car. But I've a cup left overnight. I'll have the kettle boiling in a jiffy. Would you like a nice egg with it?

BERTHA.
No, thanks.

BRIGID.
Or a nice bit of toast?

BERTHA.
No, Brigid, thanks. Just a cup of tea.

BRIGID.
[*Crossing to the folding doors.*] I won't be a moment. [*She stops, turns back and goes towards the door on the left.*] But first I must waken Master Archie or there'll be ructions.

[*She goes out by the door on the left. After a few moments* BERTHA *rises and goes over to the study. She opens the door wide and looks in. One can see a small untidy room with many bookshelves and a large writingtable with papers and an extinguished lamp and before it a padded chair. She remains standing for some time in the doorway, then closes the door again without entering the room. She returns to her chair by the window and sits* down. ARCHIE, *dressed as before, comes in by the door on the right, followed by* BRIGID.]

ARCHIE.
[*Comes to her and, putting up his face to be kissed, says:*] *Buon giorno*, mamma!

BERTHA.
[*Kissing him.*] *Buon giorno*, Archie! [*To* BRIGID.] Did you put another vest on him under that one?

BRIGID.
He wouldn't let me, ma'am.

ARCHIE.
I'm not cold, mamma.

BERTHA.
I said you were to put it on, didn't I?

ARCHIE.
But where is the cold?

BERTHA.
[*Takes a comb from her head and combs his hair back at both sides.*] And the sleep is in your eyes still.

BRIGID.
He went to bed immediately after you went out last night, ma'am.

ARCHIE.
You know he's going to let me drive, mamma.

BERTHA.
[*Replacing the comb in her hair, embraces him suddenly.*] O, what a big man to drive a horse!

BRIGID.
Well, he's daft on horses, anyhow.

ARCHIE.

[*Releasing himself.*] I'll make him go quick. You will see from the window, mamma. With the whip. [*He makes the gesture of cracking a whip and shouts at the top of his voice.*] Avanti!

BRIGID.

Beat the poor horse, is it?

BERTHA.

Come here till I clean your mouth. [*She takes her handkerchief from the pocket of her gown, wets it with her tongue and cleans his mouth.*] You're all smudges or something, dirty little creature you are.

ARCHIE.

[*Repeats, laughing.*] Smudges! What is smudges?

[*The noise is heard of a milkcan rattled on the railings before the window.*]

BRIGID.

[*Draws aside the curtains and looks out.*] Here he is!

ARCHIE.

[*Rapidly.*] Wait. I'm ready. Goodbye, mamma! [*He kisses her hastily and turns to go.*] Is pappie up?

BRIGID.

[*Takes him by the arm.*] Come on with you now.

BERTHA.

Mind yourself, Archie, and don't be long or I won't let you go any more.

ARCHIE.

All right. Look out of the window and you'll see me. Goodbye.

[BRIGID *and* ARCHIE *go out by the door on the left.* BERTHA *stands up and, drawing aside the curtains still more, stands in the embrasure of the window looking out. The hall door is heard opening: then a slight noise of voices and cans is heard. The door is closed. After a moment or two* BERTHA *is seen waving her hand gaily in a salute.* BRIGID *enters and stands behind her, looking over her shoulder.*]

BRIGID.
Look at the sit of him! As serious as you like.

BERTHA.
[*Suddenly withdrawing from her post.*] Stand out of the window. I don't want to be seen.

BRIGID.
Why, ma'am, what is it?

BERTHA.
[*Crossing towards the folding doors.*] Say I'm not up, that I'm not well. I can't see anyone.

BRIGID.
[*Follows her.*] Who is it, ma'am?

BERTHA.
[*Halting.*] Wait a moment.

[*She listens. A knock is heard at the hall door.*]

BERTHA.
[*Stands a moment in doubt, then.*] No, say I'm in.

BRIGID.
[*In doubt.*] Here?

BERTHA.
[*Hurriedly.*] Yes. Say I have just got up.

[BRIGID *goes out on the left.* BERTHA *goes towards the double doors and fingers the curtains nervously, as if settling them. The hall door is heard to open. Then* BEATRICE JUSTICE *enters and, as* BERTHA *does not turn at once, stands in hesitation near the door on the left. She is dressed as before and has a newspaper in her hand.*]

BEATRICE.
[*Advances rapidly.*] Mrs Rowan, excuse me for coming at such an hour.

BERTHA.
[*Turns.*] Good morning, Miss Justice. [*She comes towards her.*] Is anything the matter?

BEATRICE.
[*Nervously.*] I don't know. That is what I wanted to ask you.

BERTHA.
[*Looks curiously at her.*] You are out of breath. Won't you sit down?

BEATRICE.
[*Sitting down.*] Thank you.

BERTHA.
[*Sits opposite her, pointing to her paper.*] Is there something in the paper?

BEATRICE.
[*Laughs nervously: opens the paper.*] Yes.

BERTHA.
About Dick?

BEATRICE.
Yes. Here it is. A long article, a leading article, by my cousin. All his life is here. Do you wish to see it?

BERTHA.
[*Takes the paper, and opens it.*] Where is it?

BEATRICE.
In the middle. It is headed: *A Distinguished Irishman.*

BERTHA.
Is it... for Dick or against him?

BEATRICE.
[*Warmly.*] O, for him! You can read what he says about Mr Rowan. And I know that Robert stayed in town very late last night to write it.

BERTHA.
[*Nervously.*] Yes. Are you sure?

BEATRICE.
Yes. Very late. I heard him come home. It was long after two.

BERTHA.
[*Watching her.*] It alarmed you? I mean to be awakened at that hour of the morning.

BEATRICE.
I am a light sleeper. But I knew he had come from the office and then... I suspected he had written an article about Mr Rowan and that was why he came so late.

BERTHA.
How quick you were to think of that!

BEATRICE.
Well, after what took place here yesterday afternoon—I mean what Robert said, that Mr Rowan had accepted this position. It was only natural I should think...

BERTHA.
Ah, yes. Naturally.

BEATRICE.
[*Hastily.*] But that is not what alarmed me. But immediately after I heard a noise in my cousin's room.

BERTHA.
[*Crumples together the paper in her hands, breathlessly.*] My God! What is it? Tell me.

BEATRICE.
[*Observing her.*] Why does that upset you so much?

BERTHA.
[*Sinking back, with a forced laugh.*] Yes, of course, it is very foolish of me. My nerves are all upset. I slept very badly, too. That is why I got up so early. But tell me what was it then?

BEATRICE.
Only the noise of his valise being pulled along the floor. Then I heard him walking about his room, whistling softly. And then locking it and strapping it.

BERTHA.
He is going away!

BEATRICE.
That was what alarmed me. I feared he had had a quarrel with Mr Rowan and that his article was an attack.

BERTHA.
But why should they quarrel? Have you noticed anything between them?

BEATRICE.
I thought I did. A coldness.

BERTHA.
Lately?

BEATRICE.
For some time past.

BERTHA.
[*Smoothing the paper out.*] Do you know the reason?

BEATRICE.
[*Hesitatingly.*] No.

BERTHA.
[*After a pause.*] Well, but if this article is for him, as you say, they have not quarrelled. [*She reflects a moment.*] And written last night, too.

BEATRICE.
Yes. I bought the paper at once to see. But why, then, is he going away so suddenly? I feel that there is something wrong. I feel that something has happened between them.

BERTHA.
Would you be sorry?

BEATRICE.
I would be very sorry. You see, Mrs Rowan, Robert is my first cousin and it would grieve me very deeply if he were to treat Mr Rowan badly, now that he has come back, or if they had a serious quarrel especially because...

BERTHA.
[*Toying with the paper.*] Because?

BEATRICE.
Because it was my cousin who urged Mr Rowan always to come back. I have that on my conscience.

BERTHA.
It should be on Mr Hand's conscience, should it not?

BEATRICE.
[*Uncertainly.*] On mine, too. Because—I spoke to my cousin about Mr Rowan when he was away and, to a certain extent, it was I...

BERTHA.
[*Nods slowly.*] I see. And that is on your conscience. Only that?

BEATRICE.
I think so.

BERTHA.
[*Almost cheerfully.*] It looks as if it was you, Miss Justice, who brought my husband back to Ireland.

BEATRICE.
I, Mrs Rowan?

BERTHA.
Yes, you. By your letters to him and then by speaking to your cousin as you said just now. Do you not think that you are the person who brought him back?

BEATRICE.
[*Blushing suddenly.*] No. I could not think that.

BERTHA.
[*Watches her for a moment; then turning aside.*] You know that my husband is writing very much since he came back.

BEATRICE.
Is he?

BERTHA.
Did you not know? [*She points towards the study.*] He passes the greater part of the night in there writing. Night after night.

BEATRICE.
In his study?

BERTHA.
Study or bedroom. You may call it what you please. He sleeps there, too, on a sofa. He slept there last night. I can show you if you don't believe me.

[*She rises to go towards the study.* BEATRICE *half rises quickly and makes a gesture of refusal.*]

BEATRICE.
I believe you, of course, Mrs Rowan, when you tell me.

BERTHA.
[*Sitting down again.*] Yes. He is writing. And it must be about something which has come into his life lately— since we came back to Ireland. Some change. Do you know that any change has come into his life? [*She looks searchingly at her.*] Do you know it or feel it?

BEATRICE.
[*Answers her look steadily.*] Mrs Rowan, that is not a question to ask me. If any change has come into his life since he came back you must know and feel it.

BERTHA.
You could know it just as well. You are very intimate in this house.

BEATRICE.
I am not the only person who is intimate here.

[*They both look at each other coldly in silence for some moments.* BERTHA *lays aside the paper and sits down on a chair nearer to* BEATRICE.]

BERTHA.
[*Placing her hand on* BEATRICE'S *knee.*] So you also hate me, Miss Justice?

BEATRICE.
[*With an effort.*] Hate you? I?

BERTHA.
[*Insistently but softly.*] Yes. You know what it means to hate a person?

BEATRICE.
Why should I hate you? I have never hated anyone.

BERTHA.
Have you ever loved anyone? [*She puts her hand on* BEATRICE'S *wrist.*] Tell me. You have?

BEATRICE.
[*Also softly.*] Yes. In the past.

BERTHA.
Not now?

BEATRICE.
No.

BERTHA.
Can you say that to me—truly? Look at me.

BEATRICE.
[*Looks at her.*] Yes, I can.

[*A short pause.* BERTHA *withdraws her hand, and turns away her head in some embarrassment.*]

BERTHA.
You said just now that another person is intimate in this house. You meant your cousin... Was it he?

BEATRICE.
Yes.

BERTHA.
Have you not forgotten him?

BEATRICE.
[*Quietly.*] I have tried to.

BERTHA.
[*Clasping her hands.*] You hate me. You think I am happy. If you only knew how wrong you are!

BEATRICE.
[*Shakes her head.*] I do not.

BERTHA.
Happy! When I do not understand anything that he writes, when I cannot help him in any way, when I don't even understand half of what he says to me sometimes! You could and you can. [*Excitedly.*] But I am afraid for him, afraid for both of them. [*She stands up suddenly and goes towards the davenport.*] He must not go away like that. [*She takes a writing pad from the drawer and writes a few lines in great haste.*] No, it is impossible! Is he mad to do such a thing? [*Turning to* BEATRICE.] Is he still at home?

BEATRICE.
[*Watching her in wonder.*] Yes. Have you written to him to ask him to come here?

BERTHA.
[*Rises.*] I have. I will send Brigid across with it. Brigid!

[*She goes out by the door on the left rapidly.*]

BEATRICE.
[*Gazing after her, instinctively:*] It is true, then!

[*She glances toward the door of* RICHARD'S *study and catches her head in her hands. Then, recovering herself, she takes the paper from the little table, opens it, takes a spectacle case from her handbag and, putting on a pair of spectacles, bends down, reading it.* RICHARD ROWAN *enters from the garden. He is dressed as before but wears a soft hat and carries a thin cane.*]

RICHARD.

[*Stands in the doorway, observing her for some moments.*] There are demons [*he points out towards the strand*] out there. I heard them jabbering since dawn.

BEATRICE.

[*Starts to her feet.*] Mr Rowan!

RICHARD.

I assure you. The isle is full of voices. Yours also, *Otherwise I could not see you,* it said. And her voice. But, I assure you, they are all demons. I made the sign of the cross upside down and that silenced them.

BEATRICE.

[*Stammering.*] I came here, Mr Rowan, so early because... to show you this... Robert wrote it... about you... last night.

RICHARD.

[*Takes off his hat.*] My dear Miss Justice, you told me yesterday, I think, why you came here and I never forget anything. [*Advancing towards her, holding out his hand.*] Good morning.

BEATRICE.

[*Suddenly takes off her spectacles and places the paper in his hands.*] I came for this. It is an article about you. Robert wrote it last night. Will you read it?

RICHARD.

[*Bows.*] Read it now? Certainly.

BEATRICE.

[*Looks at him in despair.*] O, Mr Rowan, it makes me suffer to look at you.

RICHARD.
[*Opens and reads the paper.*] *Death of the Very Reverend Canon Mulhall.* Is that it?

[BERTHA *appears at the door on the left and stands to listen.*]

RICHARD.
[*Turns over a page.*] Yes, here we are! *A Distinguished Irishman.* [*He begins to read in a rather loud hard voice.*] Not the least vital of the problems which confront our country is the problem of her attitude towards those of her children who, having left her in her hour of need, have been called back to her now on the eve of her longawaited victory, to her whom in loneliness and exile they have at last learned to love. In exile, we have said, but here we must distinguish. There is an economic and there is a spiritual exile. There are those who left her to seek the bread by which men live and there are others, nay, her most favoured children, who left her to seek in other lands that food of the spirit by which a nation of human beings is sustained in life. Those who recall the intellectual life of Dublin of a decade since will have many memories of Mr Rowan. Something of that fierce indignation which lacerated the heart...

[*He raises his eyes from the paper and sees* BERTHA *standing in the doorway. Then he lays aside the paper and looks at her. A long silence.*]

BEATRICE.
[*With an effort.*] You see, Mr Rowan, your day has dawned at last. Even here. And you see that you have a warm friend in Robert, a friend who understands you.

RICHARD.
Did you notice the little phrase at the beginning: *those who left her in her hour of need?*

[*He looks searchingly at* BERTHA*, turns and walks into his study, closing the door behind him.*]

BERTHA.
[*Speaking half to herself.*] I gave up everything for him, religion, family, my own peace.

[*She sits down heavily in an armchair.* BEATRICE *comes towards her.*]

BEATRICE.
[*Weakly.*] But do you not feel also that Mr Rowan's ideas...

BERTHA.
[*Bitterly.*] Ideas and ideas! But the people in this world have other ideas or pretend to. They have to put up with him in spite of his ideas because he is able to do something. Me, no. I am nothing.

BEATRICE.
You stand by his side.

BERTHA.
[*With increasing bitterness.*] Ah, nonsense, Miss Justice! I am only a thing he got entangled with and my son is— the nice name they give those children. Do you think I am a stone? Do you think I don't see it in their eyes and in their manner when they have to meet me?

BEATRICE.
Do not let them humble you, Mrs Rowan.

BERTHA.
[*Haughtily.*] Humble me! I am very proud of myself, if you want to know. What have they ever done for him? I

made him a man. What are they all in his life? No more than the dirt under his boots! [*She stands up and walks excitedly to and fro.*] He can despise me, too, like the rest of them—now. And you can despise me. But you will never humble me, any of you.

BEATRICE.
Why do you accuse me?

BERTHA.
[*Going to her impulsively.*] I am in such suffering. Excuse me if I was rude. I want us to be friends. [*She holds out her hands.*] Will you?

BEATRICE.
[*Taking her hands.*] Gladly.

BERTHA.
[*Looking at her.*] What lovely long eyelashes you have! And your eyes have such a sad expression!

BEATRICE.
[*Smiling.*] I see very little with them. They are very weak.

BERTHA.
[*Warmly.*] But beautiful.

[*She embraces her quietly and kisses her. Then withdraws from her a little shyly.* BRIGID *comes in from the left.*]

BRIGID.
I gave it to himself, ma'am.

BERTHA.
Did he send a message?

BRIGID.
He was just going out, ma'am. He told me to say he'd be here after me.

BERTHA.
Thanks.

BRIGID.
[*Going.*] Would you like the tea and the toast now, ma'am?

BERTHA.
Not now, Brigid. After perhaps. When Mr Hand comes show him in at once.

BRIGID.
Yes, ma'am.

[*She goes out on the left.*]

BEATRICE.
I will go now, Mrs Rowan, before he comes.

BERTHA.
[*Somewhat timidly.*] Then we are friends?

BEATRICE.
[*In the same tone.*] We will try to be. [*Turning.*] Do you allow me to go out through the garden? I don't want to meet my cousin now.

BERTHA.
Of course. [*She takes her hand.*] It is so strange that we spoke like this now. But I always wanted to. Did you?

BEATRICE.
I think I did, too.

BERTHA.
[*Smiling.*] Even in Rome. When I went out for a walk with Archie I used to think about you, what you were like, because I knew about you from Dick. I used to look at different persons, coming out of churches or going by

in carriages, and think that perhaps they were like you. Because Dick told me you were dark.

BEATRICE.
[*Again nervously.*] Really?

BERTHA.
[*Pressing her hand.*] Goodbye then—for the present.

BEATRICE.
[*Disengaging her hand.*] Good morning.

BERTHA.
I will see you to the gate.

[*She accompanies her out through the double doors. They go down through the garden.* RICHARD ROWAN *comes in from the study. He halts near the doors, looking down the garden. Then he turns away, comes to the little table, takes up the paper and reads.* BERTHA, *after some moments, appears in the doorway and stands watching him till he has finished. He lays down the paper again and turns to go back to his study.*]

BERTHA.
Dick!

RICHARD.
[*Stopping.*] Well?

BERTHA.
You have not spoken to me.

RICHARD.
I have nothing to say. Have you?

BERTHA.
Do you not wish to know—about what happened last night?

RICHARD.
That I will never know.

BERTHA.
I will tell you if you ask me.

RICHARD.
You will tell me. But I will never know. Never in this world.

BERTHA.
[*Moving towards him.*] I will tell you the truth, Dick, as I always told you. I never lied to you.

RICHARD.
[*Clenching his hands in the air, passionately.*] Yes, yes. The truth! But I will never know, I tell you.

BERTHA.
Why, then, did you leave me last night?

RICHARD.
[*Bitterly.*] In your hour of need.

BERTHA.
[*Threateningly.*] You urged me to it. Not because you love me. If you loved me or if you knew what love was you would not have left me. For your own sake you urged me to it.

RICHARD.
I did not make myself. I am what I am.

BERTHA.
To have it always to throw against me. To make me humble before you, as you always did. To be free yourself. [*Pointing towards the garden.*] With her! And that is your love! Every word you say is false.

RICHARD.
[*Controlling himself.*] It is useless to ask you to listen to me.

BERTHA.
Listen to you! She is the person for listening. Why would you waste your time with me? Talk to her.

RICHARD.
[*Nods his head.*] I see. You have driven her away from me now, as you drove everyone else from my side—every friend I ever had, every human being that ever tried to approach me. You hate her.

BERTHA.
[*Warmly.*] No such thing! I think you have made her unhappy as you have made me and as you made your dead mother unhappy and killed her. Womankiller! That is your name.

RICHARD.
[*Turns to go.*] Arrivederci!

BERTHA.
[*Excitedly.*] She is a fine and high character. I like her. She is everything that I am not—in birth and education. You tried to ruin her but you could not. Because she is well able for you—what I am not. And you know it.

RICHARD.
[*Almost shouting.*] What the devil are you talking about her for?

BERTHA.
[*Clasping her hands.*] O, how I wish I had never met you! How I curse that day!

RICHARD.
[*Bitterly.*] I am in the way, is it? You would like to be free now. You have only to say the word.

BERTHA.
[*Proudly.*] Whenever you like I am ready.

RICHARD.
So that you could meet your lover—freely?

BERTHA.
Yes.

RICHARD.
Night after night?

BERTHA.
[*Gazing before her and speaking with intense passion.*] To meet my lover! [*Holding out her arms before her.*] My lover! Yes! My lover!

[*She bursts suddenly into tears and sinks down on a chair, covering her face with her hands.* RICHARD *approaches her slowly and touches her on the shoulder.*]

RICHARD.
Bertha! [*She does not answer.*] Bertha, you are free.

BERTHA.
[*Pushes his hand aside and starts to her feet.*] Don't touch me! You are a stranger to me. You do not understand anything in me—not one thing in my heart or soul. A stranger! I am living with a stranger!

[*A knock is heard at the hall door.* BERTHA *dries her eyes quickly with her handkerchief and settles the front of her gown.* RICHARD *listens for a moment, looks at her keenly and, turning away, walks into his study.* ROBERT HAND *enters from the left. He is dressed in dark brown and carries in his hand a brown Alpine hat.*]

ROBERT.
[*Closing the door quietly behind him.*] You sent for me.

BERTHA.
[*Rises.*] Yes. Are you mad to think of going away like that—without even coming here—without saying anything?

ROBERT.
[*Advancing towards the table on which the paper lies, glances at it.*] What I have to say I said here.

BERTHA.
When did you write it? Last night—after I went away?

ROBERT.
[*Gracefully.*] To be quite accurate, I wrote part of it—in my mind—before you went away. The rest—the worst part—I wrote after. Much later.

BERTHA.
And you could write last night!

ROBERT.
[*Shrugs his shoulders.*] I am a welltrained animal. [*He comes closer to her.*] I passed a long wandering night after... in my office, at the vicechancellor's house, in a nightclub, in the streets, in my room. Your image was always before my eyes, your hand in my hand. Bertha, I will never forget last night. [*He lays his hat on the table and takes her hand.*] Why do you not look at me? May I not touch you?

BERTHA.
[*Points to the study.*] Dick is in there.

ROBERT.
[*Drops her hand.*] In that case children be good.

BERTHA.
Where are you going?

ROBERT.
To foreign parts. That is, to my cousin Jack Justice, *alias* Doggy Justice, in Surrey. He has a nice country place there and the air is mild.

BERTHA.
Why are you going?

ROBERT.
[*Looks at her in silence.*] Can you not guess one reason?

BERTHA.
On account of me?

ROBERT.
Yes. It is not pleasant for me to remain here just now.

BERTHA.
[*Sits down helplessly.*] But this is cruel of you, Robert. Cruel to me and to him also.

ROBERT.
Has he asked... what happened?

BERTHA.
[*Joining her hands in despair.*] No. He refuses to ask me anything. He says he will never know.

ROBERT.
[*Nods gravely.*] Richard is right there. He is always right.

BERTHA.
But, Robert, you must speak to him.

ROBERT.
What am I to say to him?

BERTHA.
The truth! Everything!

ROBERT.
[*Reflects.*] No, Bertha. I am a man speaking to a man. I cannot tell him everything.

BERTHA.
He will believe that you are going away because you are afraid to face him after last night.

ROBERT.
[*After a pause.*] Well, I am not a coward any more than he. I will see him.

BERTHA.
[*Rises.*] I will call him.

ROBERT.
[*Catching her hands.*] Bertha! What happened last night? What is the truth that I am to tell? [*He gazes earnestly into her eyes.*] Were you mine in that sacred night of love? Or have I dreamed it?

BERTHA.
[*Smiles faintly.*] Remember your dream of me. You dreamed that I was yours last night.

ROBERT.
And that is the truth—a dream? That is what I am to tell?

BERTHA.
Yes.

ROBERT.
[*Kisses both her hands.*] Bertha! [*In a softer voice.*] In all my life only that dream is real. I forget the rest. [*He kisses her hands again.*] And now I can tell him the truth. Call him.

[BERTHA *goes to the door of* RICHARD'S *study and knocks. There is no answer. She knocks again.*]

BERTHA.

Dick! [*There is no answer.*] Mr Hand is here. He wants to speak to you, to say goodbye. He is going away. [*There is no answer. She beats her hand loudly on the panel of the door and calls in an alarmed voice.*] Dick! Answer me!

[RICHARD ROWAN *comes in from the study. He comes at once to* ROBERT *but does not hold out his hand.*]

RICHARD.

[*Calmly.*] I thank you for your kind article about me. Is it true that you have come to say goodbye?

ROBERT.

There is nothing to thank me for, Richard. Now and always I am your friend. Now more than ever before. Do you believe me, Richard?

[RICHARD *sits down on a chair and buries his face in his hands.* BERTHA *and* ROBERT *gaze at each other in silence. Then she turns away and goes out quietly on the right.* ROBERT *goes towards* RICHARD *and stands near him, resting his hands on the back of a chair, looking down at him. There is a long silence. A* FISHWOMAN *is heard crying out as she passes along the road outside.*]

THE   FISHWOMAN.

Fresh Dublin bay herrings! Fresh Dublin bay herrings! Dublin bay herrings!

ROBERT.

[*Quietly.*] I will tell you the truth, Richard. Are you listening?

RICHARD.

[*Raises his face and leans back to listen.*] Yes.

[ROBERT *sits on the chair beside him. The* FISHWOMAN *is heard calling out farther away.*]

THE   FISHWOMAN.
Fresh herrings! Dublin bay herrings!

ROBERT.
I failed, Richard. That is the truth. Do you believe me?

RICHARD.
I am listening.

ROBERT.
I failed. She is yours, as she was nine years ago, when you met her first.

RICHARD.
When we met her first, you mean.

ROBERT.
Yes. [*He looks down for some moments.*] Shall I go on?

RICHARD.
Yes.

ROBERT.
She went away. I was left alone—for the second time. I went to the vicechancellor's house and dined. I said you were ill and would come another night. I made epigrams new and old—that one about the statues also. I drank claret cup. I went to my office and wrote my article. Then...

RICHARD.
Then?

ROBERT.
Then I went to a certain nightclub. There were men there—and also women. At least, they looked like

women. I danced with one of them. She asked me to see her home. Shall I go on?

RICHARD.
Yes.

ROBERT.
I saw her home in a cab. She lives near Donnybrook. In the cab took place what the subtle Duns Scotus calls a death of the spirit. Shall I go on?

RICHARD.
Yes.

ROBERT.
She wept. She told me she was the divorced wife of a barrister. I offered her a sovereign as she told me she was short of money. She would not take it and wept very much. Then she drank some melissa water from a little bottle which she had in her satchel. I saw her enter her house. Then I walked home. In my room I found that my coat was all stained with the melissa water. I had no luck even with my coats yesterday: that was the second one. The idea came to me then to change my suit and go away by the morning boat. I packed my valise and went to bed. I am going away by the next train to my cousin, Jack Justice, in Surrey. Perhaps for a fortnight. Perhaps longer. Are you disgusted?

RICHARD.
Why did you not go by the boat?

ROBERT.
I slept it out.

RICHARD.
You intended to go without saying goodbye—without coming here?

ROBERT.
Yes.

RICHARD.
Why?

ROBERT.
My story is not very nice, is it?

RICHARD.
But you have come.

ROBERT.
Bertha sent me a message to come.

RICHARD.
But for that...?

ROBERT.
But for that I should not have come.

RICHARD.
Did it strike you that if you had gone without coming here I should have understood it—in my own way?

ROBERT.
Yes, it did.

RICHARD.
What, then, do you wish me to believe?

ROBERT.
I wish you to believe that I failed. That Bertha is yours now as she was nine years ago, when you—when we—met her first.

RICHARD.
Do you want to know what I did?

ROBERT.
No.

RICHARD.
I came home at once.

ROBERT.
Did you hear Bertha return?

RICHARD.
No. I wrote all the night. And thought. [*Pointing to the study.*] In there. Before dawn I went out and walked the strand from end to end.

ROBERT.
[*Shaking his head.*] Suffering. Torturing yourself.

RICHARD.
Hearing voices about me. The voices of those who say they love me.

ROBERT.
[*Points to the door on the right.*] One. And mine?

RICHARD.
Another still.

ROBERT.
[*Smiles and touches his forehead with his right forefinger.*] True. My interesting but somewhat melancholy cousin. And what did they tell you?

RICHARD.
They told me to despair.

ROBERT.
A queer way of showing their love, I must say! And will you despair?

RICHARD.
[*Rising.*] No.

[*A noise is heard at the window.* ARCHIE'S *face is seen flattened against one of the panes. He is heard calling.*]

ARCHIE.
Open the window! Open the window!

ROBERT.
[*Looks at* RICHARD.] Did you hear his voice, too, Richard, with the others—out there on the strand? Your son's voice. [*Smiling.*] Listen! How full it is of despair!

ARCHIE.
Open the window, please, will you?

ROBERT.
Perhaps, there, Richard, is the freedom we seek—you in one way, I in another. In him and not in us. Perhaps...

RICHARD.
Perhaps...?

ROBERT.
I said *perhaps*. I would say almost surely if...

RICHARD.
If what?

ROBERT.
[*With a faint smile.*] If he were mine.

[*He goes to the window and opens it.* ARCHIE *scrambles in.*]

ROBERT.
Like yesterday—eh?

ARCHIE.
Good morning, Mr Hand. [*He runs to* RICHARD *and kisses him:*] *Buon giorno, babbo.*

RICHARD.
Buon giorno, Archie.

ROBERT.
And where were you, my young gentleman?

ARCHIE.
Out with the milkman. I drove the horse. We went to Booterstown. [*He takes off his cap and throws it on a chair.*] I am very hungry.

ROBERT.
[*Takes his hat from the table.*] Richard, goodbye. [*Offering his hand.*] To our next meeting!

RICHARD.
[*Rises, touches his hand.*] Goodbye.

[BERTHA *appears at the door on the right.*]

ROBERT.
[*Catches sight of her: to* ARCHIE.] Get your cap. Come on with me. I'll buy you a cake and I'll tell you a story.

ARCHIE.
[*To* BERTHA.] May I, mamma?

BERTHA.
Yes.

ARCHIE.
[*Takes his cap.*] I am ready.

ROBERT.
[*To* RICHARD *and* BERTHA.] Goodbye to pappa and mamma. But not a big goodbye.

ARCHIE.
Will you tell me a fairy story, Mr Hand?

ROBERT.
A fairy story? Why not? I am your fairy godfather.

[*They go out together through the double doors and down the garden. When they have gone* BERTHA *goes to* RICHARD *and puts her arm round his waist.*]

BERTHA.
Dick, dear, do you believe now that I have been true to you? Last night and always?

RICHARD.
[*Sadly.*] Do not ask me, Bertha.

BERTHA.
[*Pressing him more closely.*] I have been, dear. Surely you believe me. I gave you myself—all. I gave up all for you. You took me—and you left me.

RICHARD.
When did I leave you?

BERTHA.
You left me: and I waited for you to come back to me. Dick, dear, come here to me. Sit down. How tired you must be!

[*She draws him towards the lounge. He sits down, almost reclining, resting on his arm. She sits on the mat before the lounge, holding his hand.*]

BERTHA.
Yes, dear. I waited for you. Heavens, what I suffered then—when we lived in Rome! Do you remember the terrace of our house?

RICHARD.
Yes.

BERTHA.
I used to sit there, waiting, with the poor child with his toys, waiting till he got sleepy. I could see all the roofs of the city and the river, the *Tevere*. What is its name?

RICHARD.
The Tiber.

BERTHA.
[*Caressing her cheek with his hand.*] It was lovely, Dick, only I was so sad. I was alone, Dick, forgotten by you and by all. I felt my life was ended.

RICHARD.
It had not begun.

BERTHA.
And I used to look at the sky, so beautiful, without a cloud and the city you said was so old: and then I used to think of Ireland and about ourselves.

RICHARD.
Ourselves?

BERTHA.
Yes. Ourselves. Not a day passes that I do not see ourselves, you and me, as we were when we met first. Every day of my life I see that. Was I not true to you all that time?

RICHARD.
[*Sighs deeply.*] Yes, Bertha. You were my bride in exile.

BERTHA.
Wherever you go, I will follow you. If you wish to go away now I will go with you.

RICHARD.
I will remain. It is too soon yet to despair.

BERTHA.
[*Again caressing his hand.*] It is not true that I want to drive everyone from you. I wanted to bring you close together—you and him. Speak to me. Speak out all your heart to me. What you feel and what you suffer.

RICHARD.
I am wounded, Bertha.

BERTHA.

How wounded, dear? Explain to me what you mean. I
will try to understand everything you say. In what way
are you wounded?

RICHARD.

[*Releases his hand and, taking her head between his
hands, bends it back and gazes long into her eyes.*] I have
a deep, deep wound of doubt in my soul.

BERTHA.

[*Motionless.*] Doubt of me?

RICHARD.

Yes.

BERTHA.

I am yours. [*In a whisper.*] If I died this moment, I am
yours.

RICHARD.

[*Still gazing at her and speaking as if to an absent
person.*] I have wounded my soul for you—a deep
wound of doubt which can never be healed. I can never
know, never in this world. I do not wish to know or to
believe. I do not care. It is not in the darkness of belief
that I desire you. But in restless living wounding doubt.
To hold you by no bonds, even of love, to be united with
you in body and soul in utter nakedness—for this I
longed. And now I am tired for a while, Bertha. My
wound tires me.

[*He stretches himself out wearily along the lounge.*
BERTHA *holds his hand still, speaking very softly.*]

BERTHA.

Forget me, Dick. Forget me and love me again as you
did the first time. I want my lover. To meet him, to go to

him, to give myself to him. You, Dick. O, my strange wild lover, come back to me again!

[*She closes her eyes.*]

CPSIA information can be obtained
at www.ICGtesting.com
Printed in the USA
LVHW022347160721
692960LV00019B/1809